A Fall Afternoon in the Park

SHORT STORIES

MEHRI YALFANI

Toronto, Ontario, Canada
www.inanna.ca

Copyright © 2023 Mehri Yalfani

Except for the use of short passages for review purposes, no part of this book may be reproduced, in part or in whole, or transmitted in any form or by any means, electronically or mechanically, including photocopying, recording, or any information or storage retrieval system, without prior permission in writing from the publisher or a licence from the Canadian Copyright Collective Agency (Access Copyright).

We gratefully acknowledge the support of the Canada Council for the Arts and the Ontario Arts Council for our publishing program. We also acknowledge the financial support of the Government of Canada.

Cover design: Val Fullard
Cover art: Shirin Maali

A Fall Afternoon in the Park is a work of fiction. All the characters portrayed in this book are fictitious and any resemblance to persons living or dead is purely coincidental.

Library and Archives Canada Cataloguing in Publication

Title: A fall afternoon in the park : short stories / Mehri Yalfani.
Names: Yalfānī, Mihrī, author.
Series: Inanna poetry & fiction series.
Description: Series statement: Inanna poetry & fiction
Identifiers: Canadiana (print) 20230222064 | Canadiana (ebook) 20230222099 | ISBN 9781771339339 (softcover) | ISBN 9781771339346 (EPUB) | ISBN 9781771339353 (PDF)
Classification: LCC PS8597.A47 F35 2203 | DDC C813/.54—dc23

Printed and bound in Canada

Inanna Publications and Education Inc.
210 Founders College, York University
4700 Keele Street, Toronto, Ontario, Canada M3J 1P3
Telephone: (416) 736-5356 Fax: (416) 736-5765
Email: inanna.publications@inanna.ca Website: www.inanna.ca

CONTENTS

- 1   Adam
- 11   From Here to Eternity
- 22   Her Twin
- 32   Blame
- 40   The Intellectuals
- 49   The Spring Snowstorm
- 59   Let's Read *Ulysses*
- 68   A Fall Afternoon in the Park
- 75   Rainy Day
- 84   An Apartment for Sahand
- 94   I Didn't Know Her
- 101   Someone Won, Someone lost
- 113   The Day My Mother Became Old
- 124   Adopted Child
- 129   Nazli
- 138   A Nice, Obedient, Pious Wife
- 148   Layli Without Majnoon
- 159   Ziba Sepidrooy
- 165   A Summer's Afternoon
- 168   Sadika

- 181   *Acknowledgements*

ADAM

SHE CALLED ME "ADAM," as if I didn't have a name of my own. In Farsi, "Adam" means "human being," but is also used as a generic term for an employee when the individual's name isn't known. Yes, I'm a human being, but each human has a name. Even a pet dog or cat that we keep, we call them by a name. She may not know that a name is part of our identity, and our history, and part of our family's history as well. Well, how would she know? Her father, according to other people who knew him, and also to herself, was, as she called him, "a rich idiot." That's it. No name. She didn't say more: nothing about her father or her mother, nor her sisters, nor her brothers, if she has any. She might not have considered me someone worth talking about her life with. I say for sure that she hated her father. Why? I couldn't figure it out. How could I? I knew nothing about her life. The things that I'd heard from her she uttered unintentionally. She always complained about her life, her mother and her father and everything. I guessed she hated her father because of the name he gave her, which she hated. She didn't tell me her name. Yes, she hated her rich idiot father. Sorry for using this language, but it was her fault. She provoked anger in me, not kindness. She considered me inferior to her.

I'd like to have told her, *Ms. Such and Such, because of your rich idiot father, you're living a luxurious life and I have to work for you and you call me your Adam.* I didn't know why she used this word. It's degrading. Or it might just have been my perception and I was mistaken. I didn't feel any insult in her behaviour, but she was careless. I even felt jealousy in her words; yes, there was a mixture of contrary feelings, exactly like her own character—sometimes kind and nice, and sometimes arrogant and pretentious. She might have heard something about dealing with people who come to her house to clean and she knows that she has to treat them respectfully—like human beings—and hasn't the right to insult or degrade them. She might know that this country has rules and laws.

One day she was talking on the phone to one of her friends, who might be someone like herself. I heard her saying, "Yes, today I have Adam, the one who comes once a week to clean my house." If her friend wasn't like her, she would have asked her, "This Adam doesn't have a name?"

And another time I heard her to say to one of her friends, "Her name is Setareh," and she laughed mockingly.

The first day I came to her house, she asked me, "Your name?"

I said, "Setareh," which means "star" in Farsi.

It seemed as if she didn't believe that a woman coming to her place to clean could have a nice name like Setareh. I didn't understand why my name was a problem for her. I don't know what she expected my name to be. She probably thought that it was more suitable for people who live a luxurious life like her, not someone like me with a father who was a teacher and wasn't rich, like hers. My father's treasure was books and words. For our birthdays, instead of giving us golden necklaces or rings or expensive dresses, he would recite a poem and include our names in it, and when he read it to us, it was as if we were part of the poem and could register in the words forever.

I could feel that she was envious of my name. And what was her own name?

Do you think I could figure out what her name was? No, she didn't tell me. My friend introduced her to me with her family name: Mrs. Mostashari. But I'd like to know her first name—the name her parents gave her and her sisters and brothers called her. But she didn't tell me her name when she heard mine; for a while she looked at me in amazement. Her tattooed-on eyebrows went up. With a gesture of surprise, she said, "Setareh?" I thought she would say, *What a beautiful name.* But she didn't. Staring at me, she brought down her eyebrows. Her lined lips opened with a humiliating smile and again she said, "Setareh?" As if she was saying, *This beautiful name doesn't suit you, you are just a cleaning lady.*

Even weeks later, when we got to know each other better, she still never called me by my first name. She tried not to call my name at all, as if I didn't have one. But once, yes, just once, she said, "I can't believe that you have such a name. Our generation didn't have names like yours. We had old-fashioned names."

Proudly, I told her, "My father was a man of poetry and literature. He chose beautiful names for all of his children. For me, Setareh, and for my sister, Mahtab," meaning "moonlight."

She asked, "What about your brothers, do they have—"

I didn't let her finish. I said, "Arman and Kamran." My brothers' names mean "ideal," and "happy and successful."

As if she was more curious, she asked, "And on your birth certificate?"

With the same pride, I continued, "All of us have only one name on our birth certificates, too."

She heard me but she still called me Adam, not Setareh, nor Ms. Paknejad. But when she was talking on the phone—which happened very often when I was in her house—sometimes I heard her say, "Today I have an Adam, the one who comes to clean my house." She spent half the day on the phone. She didn't care how I worked. She lay on a sofa or on the bed in her bedroom with the telephone in her hand and talked.

I never saw her wear proper clothing at home; she was always in a long flowered robe that touched the floor and hid her robust body. The first day she looked me up and down as if I were for sale and she was a buyer. I had to work two to three days a week, from nine to four or five, a heavy-duty job. All the fat on my body has gone since I started this job. If I lay on a sofa all day long and someone else did the cleaning of my house, I would be overweight, too. She might envy my body as well. I'd like very much to have talked to her to know about her life, but she never told me a thing. I didn't like to ask my friend who had introduced me to her. I didn't want to show that I was curious about her private life. To tell the truth, sometimes I felt sorry for her. As she walked around the house wearing her long robe and then lying down on a sofa, it was as if she wanted to tell me that she was carefree and happy, but there was some hidden sadness, jealousy, or maybe stupidity in her face.

To tell the truth, if I did not know this lady, I wouldn't think about people's names and how they can be so important. When I was in school, some girls changed their names to something that they liked more; their families mostly accepted the new name and the old one existed just on their birth certificate. Whenever they were called they did not have to be upset by hearing the name they didn't like. I imagine this dislike of your name was a problem of the young: When you are older you don't bother yourself with this kind of unimportant matter. When we're mature, what's the difference what your name is? Your children don't call you by your first name and your family and friends are used to your name.

But when you immigrate to another country, and you make new friends, you have to introduce yourself anywhere you go, and here everybody is called by her or his first name and they pronounce it in a different way. So it is too embarrassing if you have to repeat your name often, especially the name you never liked.

I think this woman envied my name, but not my life. I went to clean her house once or twice a week and sometimes I helped her if she had a gathering in her house. She looked down on me. She never chatted with me. When she let me take a break, and she knew she had to, because of the laws in this country, she hid herself in her bedroom. That way she didn't have to exchange a few words with me and hear me tell her that I was somebody in my own country as well. I had a place of my own. I worked in a bank. I was the head of a department. I don't want to say I was a very important person, but I wasn't nobody. I raised two children and because of my children, I uprooted from my homeland and immigrated to this country.

Well, normally among Iranian families, children are the first priority, and I don't regret immigrating. So I don't talk about it. Here, I did my best to find a job to match my education and my experience but it didn't happen. Well, sometimes it doesn't. I mean, for me it didn't. I couldn't take courses and start studying again. It was too expensive and I had to make money. Yes, one of my friends found this job for me. She had the same job, working for another rich woman. She was an accountant, too. She wasn't able to find a job in her field, either. When she found out I was looking for a job, she introduced me to an agency. I worked for a while for that company. They sent me to people's houses, people who worked and had good incomes. They did not have the time or energy to clean their houses. There, no one called me Adam. Yes, they pronounced my name in a different way but it didn't bother me. I, too, might pronounce their names in a different way.

For a while I didn't tell anyone—I mean, my close Iranian friends—what I was doing. Not because I was ashamed, no. If I had told them, I wouldn't feel ashamed. But I would have felt troubled if they looked down on me. And because of that I didn't tell anyone except Parvin, my very close friend. She is a very understanding person. When she heard about it, her behaviour toward me didn't change. I noticed sympathy and surprise in her eyes. As if she was saying, *Good for you. Why not?* And, *You need to work to run the wheel of your life.*

Farhad was able to find a job in his field—I mean, accounting—but his income wasn't enough. Paying rent and all the other expenses for a family with two teenage boys can't be managed on one income. And because of that I found this cleaning job. It's hard but it brings in money.

When Parvin found out that I worked for an agency and that they took part of my income—I mean, a considerable part of my wage—she found this job for me, that is, cleaning this woman's house. She said she knew her, that she is one of those Iranians who's extremely rich and yet very generous.

Yes, true, she was generous. Sometimes she paid me more than my wage. Sometimes she sent me home early. It happened once or twice that she wanted to give me the leftover foods to take home, but I didn't accept. No, I couldn't accept any food. You might say that's meaningless pride. I know that many people, perhaps half of the world's population, don't have access to such food, or perhaps many people in this country, as well, and if they were offered it they would accept it with pleasure. But not me, I didn't want it. Our famous poet the great Saadi said, and my father always used to read it to us: "*Oh, the stubborn stomach, be happy with a piece of bread, not to be forced to bend your back to give service to someone else.*"

Yes, I had bent my back but only to earn a piece of bread. I mean, the *minimum*, which in this country is not the same minimum that Saadi means.

I told you this lady's behaviour hurt me. I didn't say anything about it to Farhad and my children. I was sure if I had told them, they would have said, *Quit your job. Don't let her insult you.* Farhad used to be a supporter of the working class. He still is, but he doesn't know exactly how to define the working class in this country.

Yes, if I told Farhad that this woman's behaviour hurts me, I know he'd start to talk about the bourgeoisie and their characteristics, that all of them are arrogant and they exploit the working class, and if I asked him what I should do so that she wouldn't call me Adam, he probably would say, *Haven't you a name? She has no right to insult you. She has to respect your human dignity.*

And I would ask him, *Is it an insult if she calls me Adam?*

No, I didn't say anything to Farhad about my problem at work. I knew he would make it worse. I had to think about it myself and find a solution. I didn't know what her reaction would be if I looked straight in her eyes and told her, *Dear lady, I have a name. My name is Setareh. What is your problem with this name?* She might have felt ashamed and apologized to me. Or she might have screamed at me, *Hey, leave my house right away. I can't stand people who are rude and want to bully me. I don't want you to work here. Keep your name for yourself and hang it on your neck like an insignia.*

ADAM

My sensitivity about my name started when I got to know this woman; otherwise, I didn't brag about my name or be proud of it. But that she wouldn't call me by my name and just called me Adam made me so frustrated.

Yes, I'd like to have gone to her bedroom and screamed at her, *Good woman, Ms. Such-and-Such or any fucking name that you have, I have a name. My name is Setareh. Do you understand: Setareh*! But I didn't dare do such thing. Well, it was clear. I was afraid to lose my job. I talked about it just to Parvin. I felt hot in my face. Sometimes with tears in my eyes and a lump in my throat, I asked Parvin, "Why does she call me Adam? Don't I have a name?"

Parvin, with a serene and soothing face, said, "Don't take it so hard. Adam is not a bad name. You are an Adam, aren't you?"

I said, "Yes, I'm an Adam, but I have a name. She calls me Adam as if she's humiliating me, as if she's calling me an illiterate rural maid."

With blame in her eyes, Parvin said, "Ms. Setareh, these words you used, I mean 'illiterate' and 'rural maid,' are negative. A maid is a person who works in other people's houses."

I said, "So, I'm no better than Mrs. Mostashari?"

Parivn looked at me and said nothing. But in her eyes there was confirmation. Yes, I'm the same kind of prejudiced person. But all these facts and Parvin's blame don't lessen the pain of being called Adam.

Parvin said, "If you really are hurt by this word, don't go to her place anymore."

"I can't not go."

"Why?"

"I need the money, and sometimes I feel pity for her."

In fact, feeling pity for Mrs. Mostashari was worth more than the money I needed. I could make money from other places, but I felt Mrs. Mostashari was a very lonely, very miserable, and very depressed woman. As if she had no one to talk to. Yes, very often she would throw a party and fill her house with Adams. Not the Adam she calls me but the Adams, as she calls them, respectable and important. Yes, she used to say, "All of them were well-known and were somebody in their own country and even still are in this country, too. They hire their Adams from this country."

And then with sadness in her voice, as if she had forgotten she was talking to me, she would continue, "Of course, the ones who know the language of this country."

And then when she realized she was talking to me, she stopped. Yes, she hasn't learned to speak the language here.

She might not need to learn it. Learning a new language isn't an easy task. I guess she was not a good student at school, and she didn't need to be, and her parents didn't care, either. She probably graduated from high school with difficulty—with the help of private tutors or her father bribing the teachers and principal of the school. She probably didn't have the grades to receive her high school diploma when she got married and went to Europe for her honeymoon.

She did not tell me all this, but when she talked on the phone with a friend, I sneaked close by to listen. She talked about her trips to Europe, to the U.S., Mexico. Her husband also has a foot here and one in another corner of the world. Whenever I asked her about him, she said, "He's on a trip."

It was none of my business that she was very wealthy and at the same time very stupid. I worked for her and she gave me my wages. Yes, sometimes she paid more. Sometimes twice my rate. And sometimes on the weekend, when I went to help when she had a party and I stayed until late at night, she sent me home in a taxi and paid me double or even more. She always left the money in an envelope. It never happened that she put the money in my hand. No, I don't complain about it.

But once I was very upset. I had been working for her for more than a year and had mentioned several times that my name was Setareh. She had said, "Yes, I know. You've told me before." Or she just said nothing. As if she hadn't heard me. One day I was angry and upset. The whole day she had hidden herself in her room and spent her time on the phone or watching Turkish TV shows in Farsi on her big TV screen on the wall. I opened the door to her bedroom several times to tell her that I had finished my job and wanted to go home, but she ignored me. She was just absorbed in the show, as if she didn't hear or see me. I left without saying goodbye to her. At night I told everything to Farhad.

Farhad still has the same ideology he had ten, twenty years ago and he still identifies a working class in his mind, which I haven't been able to do in this country. Well, I am one of those! But I don't belong to a union and can't go on strike. When Farhad heard my story, he was so angry that his neck veins swelled up and in a broken voice he said, "This lady is one of those fanatic bourgeois. But whoever she is, she has no right to insult you."

I said, "She didn't insult me; she just doesn't call me by my name. And today she hid herself in her bedroom the whole day, busy talking on the phone or watching TV, as if I didn't exist, or as if I was a machine working for her."

Farhad said, "You shouldn't go to her place anymore. We'll lodge a complaint about her."

I said, "A complaint?"

"Yes, a complaint. There are rules and laws in this country. All people are equal in the face of the law."

"But this is a capitalist country."

"That's not important. We have to lodge a complaint and take her to court."

"Where will we find the money for a lawyer?"

"We'll think about it."

We didn't file a complaint. What complaint?

Parvin said, "Don't make trouble for yourself."

But I quit my job and didn't go to her place anymore. Parvin brought me my wages for the last day I worked for Mrs. Mostashari.

Now, I'm back to my old job, working for an agency. Instead of two or three days per week, I have to work four or five days or sometimes five or six and still make less money than I made in that woman's house. I see the owners of the houses only in the morning, when I arrive. No one in these houses calls me Adam. The whole day it's just me and I feel dead tired from the hard work of cleaning. Sometimes I feel I want to cry, not from fatigue but, ironically, from my destiny and from thinking about Mrs. Mostashari, whose first name I never found out, I mean the one that her parents gave her and called her by. Or was she happy with her immense wealth and all those trips, and going and coming?

But my perception was that she wasn't happy, not because of her wealth, nor her husband and children, whom I never met. I'm not even sure if she had children but she did have so many friends and acquaintances, though she spent a lot of time talking on the phone when she wasn't watching those Turkish TV shows. In spite of all these things, I sometimes felt pity for her and sometimes I missed her.

When I talked about this to Farhad, he said, "That fanatic bourgeois? Don't think about her. Now you have your dignity, you have a name, an identity."

Yes, I have my dignity, but I don't like my job.

FROM HERE TO ETERNITY

> We, the why-less living
>   They, those who died, knowing why
>   —Ahmad Shamloo

In memory of Shohreh Yalfani
and all those who lost their lives for freedom

Soraya asked me, "Have you seen Mahin Parastooie recently?"

I said, "No, I haven't. Something happened?"

She said, "No, nothing happened. I wanted to invite her. I thought she might talk about how she lost her two sons and you could make a story out of it."

I said, "I don't need to listen to people's memories for writing a story. My stories are out of my imagination."

"But reality is always part of a story," she said.

I know she's right. I said nothing.

A few days later, I saw Mahin Parastooie at Shabnam and Iraj's place. I knew her from afar, had met her at a few gatherings, but I wasn't a close friend of hers. I had just heard about her from different people. She is in her seventies, of medium height, and seemed very fragile. Her gaze usually fixes far away, as if she's taking refuge behind her silence. I knew that she had lost her two sons in 1988 when the government wanted to eradicate all its opponents, even those who were in the prisons.

It was in Shabnam and Iraj's house that Mahin Parastooie told us the story of the loss of her sons. I'd known Shabnam and Iraj for years but I had never met Mahin Parastooie in their house. Soraya said, "I asked Shabnam to invite her and I'd like you, too, to be in our gathering." I asked Soraya, "Why are you interested in my stories? Do you think that publishers are lining up at my door to publish my works? If I tell you that right now I have several collections of short stories and novels in my desk and no publisher is interested in bringing them out, will you leave me alone?"

When she was young, Soraya had wished to be a writer but instead, life had forced her to become a hairdresser. She said, "Don't bring down your work's value. If people aren't interested in your writing, it's not your fault, it's the fault of the people who lost the way to the house of Kaaba."

I said, "If I didn't have you as a supporter, I would have kissed pen and paper goodbye and forgotten about writing. You are the only one who always encourages me and gives me hope to keep my pen green."

She said, "As long as I live, you should continue to write."

Iraj and Shabnam are the type of people whose house is a place for friends to gather. Iraj plays the tar and Shabnam has a wonderful voice. They have twin sons: one plays drum and the other, santoor. Shabnam and Iraj's parties have the true taste and colour of Iranian gatherings. When I am there I feel as if I'm in the centre of Iran. Only when the younger generations speak English or in the middle of winter you look outside and see the piles of snow do you remember that you are in Canada, thousands of kilometres away from your homeland. Soraya says, "Without this fake happiness, life in exile looks like living in Alexander the Great's prison."

Before Mahin Parastooie arrives, Shabnam said, "I haven't invited many people. Just Farzaneh and Masood, you, Soraya, and her. I thought because it's the first time that Mrs. Parastooie is coming to our place, I didn't want to have a crowded party. I thought she might not feel comfortable with people she doesn't know."

Soraya said, "I'm very interested in knowing about her children and how she lost them. If Farzaneh encourages her to talk about them, then Minoo might be able to write a story based on her account."

I said, "Soraya, leave me alone, please. I told you, I don't need people's stories."

Shabnam said, "You know that Farzaneh has finished her Ph.D. in psychology and can see clients. If Mrs. Parastooie ..."

Soraya said, "That's a good idea."

I said, "But in the presence of strangers?"

Soraya said, "She won't start her psychotherapy right here, for sure."

I told Soraya, "Please, don't give her any advice. Just let Farzaneh do her job."

At seven thirty, all the guests arrived. Mahin Parastooie came before Masood and Farzaneh. Her daughter, the only child who had been left to her and the one who had brought her to Canada, had given her a ride. Shabnam went to the door and asked her daughter to come in, but she excused herself, saying she should go home. She told her mother to call her when she wanted to go back home, but Shabnam assured her that she would send her mother back with a friend who lived in their area.

After having a dinner of a few kinds of Iranian dishes, it was time for our souls' feeding. Shabnam sang a song, while Iraj, Mahan and Bijan accompanied her on their instruments. While I was elevated by the lyrics and music, I was still thinking of Mahin Parastooie and her two young sons. Once in a while I looked at her—she was blinking constantly and her slim lips were pressed together. Her silence seemed mostly a kind of absent-mindedness, as if she was drowned in her own reveries.

A single piece of Iranian music played in Dashti spread such a sorrow among the group that my eyes filled with tears. After this melancholy selection, we discussed how Iranian music mostly expresses lamenting. Then Soraya, with her intelligence and her ingenuity, talked to Farzaneh and discussed with her depression and how we can overcome it. She cleverly made us talk about our pains in a way that all of us felt comfortable to speak of them in front of the others.

Farzaneh started, saying, "You may not believe me, but the reason that I studied psychology was a fear that I had from a young age and it didn't leave me alone for years. It was almost two years after the revolution when the government started to be very repressive. The veil was obligatory for women, and when I wanted to go to school, my mother repeated several times to be careful about my hijab because she was afraid that I might be arrested because of being careless with it. Anyway, one day when I left school to go home I was talking and laughing with my friends. I remember we were making fun of our religious teacher, who was an old clergyman who didn't feel comfortable looking in the girls' eyes. He always advised us, 'My dear daughters, have fear of satanic thoughts.' Anyway, we were just joking and laughing.

"When we reached the street where I lived, I separated from the others. Suddenly, I noticed a man close to me. In a flash, he covered my eyes and told me if I made a noise, he would kill me with a bullet. Then he forced me to get into a car. My heart beat fast in my chest and my mind went blank. I had heard about rape and execution in the prisons, but I was nobody, not a political activist. In the beginning of the revolution I was a partisan of a leftist group, but it had been more than a year since I had any contact with them, and even when I was with them, I only distributed some newspapers for them, nothing more. I felt it was all over for me and I remembered my mother, my father, my little sister, and I started to cry. One of them ridiculed me. Then I don't know what happened—I heard a voice in the car, I think they received an order to go to an assignment. Suddenly, they let me out of the car and disappeared. When I was in the street, I was happy at first, but then I was panicked that they might come back and shoot me. I didn't know where I was, I just imagined I was very far from home, in the north of Tehran where there were big houses.

"A car stopped in front of me and the driver asked me where did I need to go. I got in the car crying, without thinking that this one might be the same as the first one. But the driver was an old man who asked me, 'Have you lost your way home?' Crying, I told him what had happened to me. I said, 'I'm nobody but I don't know what happened, that they let me free and drove away.' He said, 'It was a miracle. My dear daughter, you were lucky. If they had kidnapped you, God only knows what would have happened to you. Be careful not to be alone in the street.' I said I had just been going home from school. The man shook his head with regret and said, 'Only God helps the young people in this country.'

"From then on, I didn't go to school by myself. I didn't tell the story to my parents, because I knew that then they wouldn't let me go to school anymore. But I told them that it had happened to one of my friends. So every morning my father gave me a ride on his way to work and in the afternoon, the mother of one of my classmates who lived close to us gave me a ride home. That year my parents applied to immigrate to Canada and when I got my high school diploma, we learned we had been accepted. But during those two years when we were waiting for the answer, there wasn't a single night when I wouldn't have a nightmare about being arrested in the street and taken to Evin.

"The worst thing was when I told my friends about my arrest, they believed that the men hadn't wanted to arrest me because of any political offence but because they wanted to take me out of the city and rape me, kill me, or maybe set me on fire so as not to be recognizable. Later on, during the unrest about the elections, my nightmare came back, when I heard the story of Taraneh Mosavie, who had been kidnapped in the street while she was going to a hairdresser's, and taken to the outskirts of the city, raped, then set on fire."

After a short period of silence, Soraya started to talk.

She said, "We were a bunch of children more or less the same age who went hiking with our parents, who were friends from the university. When we got older, we decided to go by ourselves, so we would be able to hike higher and also be free from their parental advice in risky situations. Anyway, on one of these trips, we hiked a considerable way and were looking at the city of Tehran from a height, with its polluted air. We were enchanted to breathe such pure air in the mountains.

"Then one of the boys started to sing the song 'Sar Amad Zemestan'—that was a leftist song that was sung during the revolution. Then the rest of the group sang with him. We sang the song to the end and had started to sing it again when a group of Pasdars appeared and blocked our way. We were a group of ten, six boys and four girls. Shadi, my sister, was in her last year of law school at Tehran University and she always assured us that if we were arrested, she could be our lawyer and acquit us very quickly. But though most of us weren't politically active, it turned out that Shadi's words really had been more of a joke—she wasn't able to get us released. Instead, the Pasdars took us to a committee and kept us there for a few days without letting us phone our parents. Among us there was a boy, Mortaza, who was active in a leftist group, and that made our case more complicated. To keep this short, at that time, I was sixteen and the youngest one among them. My father was able to get a letter from a clergyman who was somebody in the government, and with our family house as bail, I was released. But Shadi stayed in Evin without telling my parents why they kept her in prison. Their only reason was that Shadi was very stubborn and didn't want to cooperate. One of her cellmates told me later that she was a source of joy and laughter for the prisoners. She always had a very happy and positive attitude and her slogan was 'Take it easy.'

"After a few years, they called my parents to Evin and gave them Shadi's will and her belongings. This news was so unexpected for my mother that she had a stroke, and a few months later, she passed away, and whenever I called and asked about Shadi, my father just said, we are waiting or we'll see. Actually the news about this mass murder never came out in Iranian newspapers as it had for those who were executed during the 1980s—their names were in the government's newspaper. This had been a massacre and they didn't want to make it public. Then I heard the news from one of my friends who lived in Germany."

Soraya's story was so painful that we were silent for a while. Then it was my turn to tell my story. I said that compared to them, I didn't know what I could talk about. I hadn't lost any of my close family or relatives in the revolution or prison. My family was from old feudal stock and during the last government had become merchants. As my father used to say, "We had been promoted from feudalism to capitalism." I knew that my grandfather was from a city in the west of Iran, and the owner of a few villages. He sent all his sons to Tehran to study at the university. I suppose all of them had the genes of their father and had been able to accumulate a good deal of wealth. As folks say, they didn't forget how to make money. But me, I hadn't inherited any of those genes from my family and I was always happy with what I had.

I stopped talking when Soraya said, "But you're supposed to share with us a sad or painful memory if you have any."

I didn't like to talk about my past. Or as psychologists say, to talk about my complexes, but suddenly, as if there was a spark in my mind, I remembered my last year in high school.

I said, "One day, the principal came to our literature class and told us about an essay competition, saying that the winner would be taken on a trip to Isfahan and Shiraz with other winning students, and also her essay would be published in a journal to which she would receive a free year's subscription. Anyway, I was so excited that I started to think about the different subjects they might give us to write about. But when the day of the competition arrived and we were given the subject, for me it might as well have required that I grow a horn on my head. The topic wasn't the great poets' poetry or any other of the usual subjects that we had written about before. Instead, they asked us to write about the positive and negative characteristics of our teaching staff. For me, it was as if we were being forced to spy on our teachers and it was some kind of inquisition. I decided several times to give them a blank paper and quit. But then I thought that might make it harder for myself. I spent half of my time thinking about how to write and what kind of language to use. Finally I chose to write in a way that, as folks say, was neither skewer burn nor kabab. For example, I admired the principal in one sentence and in another I mentioned one of her weak traits. In this way, I didn't pound one teacher completely nor just praise her or him. In short, I walked a narrow road and tried not to put my feet out of line. But when I got the best mark for my essay, I realized there is a half bowl under the full one, as the saying goes.

"A few days later, the principal called me to the office. First she praised my essay and then she gave me a mission to make friends with as many students as I could and find out about their lives and the way they were thinking and which political group they were interested in or active in. I realized why they chose me. It wasn't because of my essay but because of my reputation as a good student and a good athlete—they thought that other students might trust me and tell me about their hidden lives. I was scared and told the story to my parents. My father was able to get a note from a famous doctor that I had a medical problem and was excused from going to school. Then they sent me away to live with my aunt. After a few months, I was sent out of the country and now I'm here with you. But living far from my family in exile pushed me to take refuge in writing. My stories mostly are the creations of my imagination. I don't want there to be any similarity between my characters and real people."

Even though my story wasn't as painful as Soraya's, it seemed to me that no one expected me to have such an experience that it forced my parents to take a risk and send me out of the country with a smuggler.

Silence fell on us for a while, then Masood said, "The fact is that we are here because life in Iran was getting unbearable or in some way dangerous and we all had no choice except to leave our homeland and take refuge in a safe country. And we all had more or less a similar experience in the new society—we had to start from square one and being integrated into the new society wasn't an easy task. It took years of struggle and hard work, especially for people who weren't young. It wasn't easy for them to start from the end of the line after we'd had a stable life in our homeland ..."

Masood was talking about subjects we had already heard about many times on many occasions. Soraya had to ask Mahin Parastooie to tell us her story before Masood and Iraj dominated the talking.

Mahin Parastooie had been quiet while the others were telling their stories. Her eyes drifted from this one to that one, and it wasn't clear whether she had listened to them or not. But when Farzaneh echoed Soraya's words, Mahin started to cry, and we watched her with respect and let her cry for as long as she wanted. But then her tears stopped abruptly, as if she had realized the sorrow of others in relation to hers wasn't worth mentioning.

Mahin Parastooie's voice was fragile; the same *sorrow* that was evident in her eyes was in her voice, too.

"My great sorrow started with the revolution and still continues."

I knew that the revolution had taken her two sons, but I didn't know the details.

Mahin Parastooie looked at us one by one, as if she wanted to find out from our faces how her first sentence had affected us. Then she continued, "All of you probably remember the year of unrest in Iran. Everyone who had had a child in the university remembered it well. You couldn't find a student who wasn't involved with politics. There was a wave that dragged them toward it. If a young one didn't go with the wave, he or she didn't have a place among them. Being involved in politics was prestigious for them. But when the new government became established, they started to eradicate anyone who said anything against them, even the ones who had helped them during the revolution. I mean they eradicated their opposition, mostly educated and young, sending them to prisons, torturing them and executing them, group by group, without any mercy. My own boys were two victims. Imagine, my Paymon wasn't even fifteen. He still didn't have a full beard and moustache. My Pirooz was a student in the Tehran Medical School. During the revolution he stayed in the hospital for weeks and gave his own blood to people who had been injured. He asked his father and me to go to the hospital to donate our blood and asked our relatives and friends to donate their blood as well. He used to say, 'The revolution needs blood.'

"When Pirooz had to leave the hospital and live in secret, they came for Paymon. I was sure that Paymon wasn't active in any leftist group. He might have distributed some newspapers that Pirooz had given him. At home, he helped Nazli in math and got some money from his father and gave it all to the group that Pirooz was a member of, or just a supporter of. They didn't tell us anything about their activities."

Mahin Parastooie looked at us individually again, as if she wanted to find out from our faces and our eyes what impression she was having on us. And then she continued, "It was the beginning of the winter. We didn't have any news from Pirooz for two weeks. He had warned us not to look for him, to let him be lost, not to risk being arrested ourselves. He had told us in a vague language that if he were arrested, he would be executed for sure. The night that they raided our house, first I thought they were looking for Pirooz, but the moment they entered our house, they blindfolded Paymon and a guard with a Kalashnikov stood in front of him. They told his father, me, and Nazli not to move. I was trembling like a tree in a storm and I asked myself, what are they going to do with my child? But my tongue was like a piece of wood. I couldn't even tell his father, *You ask them. Tell them that our child is nobody*. But I was paralyzed.

"It took an hour or two for them to search the house. All books, notebooks and newspapers that they thought might be evidence of a crime they put into a few plastic bags, and then they told Paymon, let's go. But Paymon was like a dead person; he didn't move, and his eyes were fixed on something outside the window. One of the Pasdars lifted his gun to strike Paymon, but before he brought it down, a lightning bolt flashed outside the big window and then a huge crack of thunder shook the whole building. Even though

I passed out before the strike hit my Paymon, I witnessed that he became one with the lightning, disappearing into the vast sky, becoming part of eternity.

"I don't know how the story reached Pirooz. I believe he was coming home to find out about Paymon. When I heard the sound of the doorbell, I rushed to the door. I used to recognize the sound of him pressing the doorbell: many short rings. When I opened the door, I hugged him. He said, 'I guess they are following me.' It was true. A few big men with machine guns in their hands entered our alley. Pirooz started to run and I hadn't closed the door yet when I heard the sound of a barrage. But I didn't hear any cry. I was glad that Pirooz escaped from them. At the same moment, a lightning bolt lit the whole neighbourhood and split the sky, followed by a huge thunderstorm that mingled with the sound of the barrage. I was sure that my Pirooz had also mingled with the lightning and gone to eternity."

Mahin Parastooie didn't say any more and in silence we looked at her as if she wasn't the person who had told us the story of the loss of her sons, but as if she was only a shadow of Mahin Parastooie, who comforted herself with these illusions.

When our silence had lasted for a while, it was again Mahin Parastooie who spoke.

"While I was in Iran and my husband was still living, every year he took me to the graves of Pirooz and Paymon, who had been buried close to each other. My sister and brothers and some of their friends were there, too, but I never believed my sons were sleeping under those stones with their names and the dates of their births and deaths written on them. My Pirooz and Paymon have gone to eternity, and we are here …"

HER TWIN

> Life is a beautiful custom.
> —Sohrab Sepehri

*S*IX YEARS, FIVE MONTHS AND THREE DAYS after being hired, she was handed a lay-off form. It was a spring day. The trees, after a cold winter, were green again and the city had put on a new face. Roxi was riding in a bus along an empty street, near her favourite park. A hope was sprouting in her heart: *I wish I didn't have to go to work. I would get off here and stay the morning, even the afternoon, among these trees.* In this open space, where trees surrounded the park like a wall, the grass was green. The sky a blue so deep, so even. Moments later the bus passed by the park. Here and there, scattered buildings, trees and passing vehicles were once more in sight. Roxi forgot all about her unattainable desire. She thought about her long day ahead. The open book lay forgotten in her lap. She already felt tired. The nightmare of unemployment was like a dark cloud in the sky of her mind. She couldn't make it go away.

She had been working in that factory for more than six years. She knew the entire place like her own home. She had developed an affiliation for it, a feeling which once in a while was transformed into hatred. At least she was happy that she had a job, some income. She was able to spend her own money and this gave her some pride and satisfaction. She knew her job so well that she could do it with her eyes closed. If only the nightmare of the machine would leave her alone, she might have worked with her eyes closed. The nightmare kept her on her toes. She wouldn't let anything go wrong. Her supervisor and the general manager were happy with her. She hadn't had a raise in two years, but their reasons were probably valid: economic crisis, etc., etc. And she didn't complain. In fact, nobody complained. That was it. No place for any change. The giant automatic machine that was supposed to replace them was silencing them.

She had heard about the giant machine the first day she started working. When she came in for her interview. Mr. Spencer, whom everybody called Frank (Roxi did the same, following the example of others), told her that the factory had ordered a huge machine that labelled the bottles. "Your employment is temporary." He had added: "No one can say when the machine will come. There is no way of telling."

Roxi had started her work with fear and anxiety. The supervisor, who was a middle-aged man from South Asia and had lived in this country for years, would remind her at every occasion that she should be careful, and not make any mistake. His accent was thick and it was hard for Roxi, who was a newcomer in that time, to understand him. He would send out a trail of words, and Roxi would look at him, silent and intimidated. She would think he was talking about the automatic machine.

The woman who was working beside her, Natasha, was from Romania. She was middle-aged, white and non-talkative. She would put the bottles that Roxi had labelled into the box. She always worked with her back to Roxi and she never dared to look or talk to her. During lunch, Natasha would sit with her husband who looked younger than her. They would talk a language that Roxi didn't understand. Natasha reminded her of Natasha in *War and Peace*. But this Natasha was much different from Tolstoy's Natasha, sombre and heavy.

The first few weeks and months passed quickly. Roxi being absorbed in her work, being careful not to make mistakes. She was in a world of her own. Bottles were coming to her hands like little mechanical men, and they would escape like little genies, sometimes slipping through her fingers. But most of the items she grabbed and labelled. Gradually she became faster and better. She could finally take those little magical bottles. She could start to let her thoughts wander and work only with her hands. She was able to leave the factory behind, go home, walk around, visit her past and sometimes she would go so far away that when she returned she would ask herself in surprise, *Reyhaneh are you still there?*

Rayhaneh?

Have you forgotten your own name? Aren't you Reyhaneh?

It was during the first weeks that she had to ... She didn't have to ... But then again for George, that Taiwanese supervisor who could not pronounce Reyhaneh, she had to change her name. She talked about it to Nader.

Nader told her: "It cannot be. Are you saying that we have to change our names? They call me Naider. It's their problem, not mine. I am Nader."

Rayhaneh smiled mischievously and said, "Last night when you were talking to Sam, you called yourself Naider."

"I had to."

"I have to too. I have to change my name for George. So my name will be easier to pronounce for him."

Then she realized without anybody telling her that George was probably not his real name either. She had heard many names from those countries and none of them resembled George or anything like it.

That night they sat up late and thought about different names. Nader would not accept her point, he made fun of her and when he saw that she didn't pay attention to his argument, he gave up.

"It's none of their business," he declared. "It's your name. Do whatever you want to with it."

Rayhaneh reasoned that if she didn't change her name, they might fire her. There was no reason why they couldn't. They would get somebody with an easier name, a name they could pronounce.

Later on in bed, she stayed awake thinking about different names. She wanted to find one that she liked. She thought of many names, names she had heard in this country, or had read in books: Lisa, Sue Ann. She laughed at this last one. No, she wouldn't choose that one. She liked names like Nancy, Margaret, Arline, and Anna. That reminded her of the book *Anna Karenina*.

She thought of herself as Anna, Anna … It had a nice ring to it. But it wouldn't suit her. All names were foreign to her. It was past two o'clock in the morning, but she couldn't find a name that she liked. She thought about her parents, why had they chosen that name for her? It was a beautiful name. Since she was a little girl, each time she had introduced herself, everybody had said that it was very charming. She was sure that her name was beautiful. But from the first day, she had problems with it in this country. Somewhere between being asleep and awake she remembered Roxana, one of her classmates in the last year of high school. She was from Soviet Azerbaijan. She had green eyes and golden-brown hair. Roxana played the piano. She even performed at the party at the end of the year. Those songs had lit a fire in Reyhaneh's heart. Reyhaneh had become friends with her. She went to her home several times and listened to her melodies on the piano. Roxana died the following year from blood cancer. And now years had passed since then. And Roxana was still nesting in Reyhaneh's memory with her pleasant music and the beautiful melody of her name. She had decided to name her daughter, if she ever had one, after Roxana. Her Roxana was never born.

She had her name. In the morning, when she woke up, the first thing she said to Nader was:

"I found the name I was looking for, Roxana."

Nader who was ready to leave the house, said, "You know best."

She woke her son up to go to school. He was in grade eight.

He had to stay awake at night and study for hours, so he would catch up in his English. Nader was helping him in his studies. She, too, would sometimes look up the meaning of some words for him in the dictionary, hoping that this way she might add to her own vocabulary, but when days later you asked her the meaning she could not remember it.

She didn't say a word to Peimaan about her decision to change her name. Although she had convinced herself that in order to keep her job, she had no choice but to do so. There was some kind of shame creeping inside her and she didn't want to talk about it.

Only in the factory, she said to herself.

And now after six years and five months and three days, although she was called Roxi only in the factory, Reyhaneh had been transformed into Roxi. As if she had been dissolved from one body into another. At home when Peimaan and Nader called her Reyhaneh, the name seemed strange to her. Years ago Reyhaneh had been the most beautiful and suitable name she could think of. Now this name was abandoned. Eight hours of her day, she was called Roxi, and the rest of the day …

Nader had opened a pizzeria and Peimaan went to a college in another city, and nobody was at home to call her Reyhaneh. And now …

She put on her uniform and walked toward her work station. She felt that the factory was breathing in painful silence. The workers looked at her, serious, with no smiles on their faces. They all stared at each other in unspoken fear. George gave her a letter. Roxi read the letter and immediately understood that she was being laid off and the factory would close. She looked at the worker beside her who was a young man from Bangladesh who had changed his name from Zolfaghar to Zol. He looked at her questioning eyes with a sad smile, as if to say, *We are doomed, we are all doomed.* "What about the automatic machine?" Roxi asked. If she had heard that the automatic machine had finally arrived, she would probably not be as shocked that the factory was to be shut.

It was like the news of the death of a loved one. The manager of the factory who was a giant Canadian man, entered the area.

Everybody called him Mr. Smith. Mr. Smith gathered the factory workers in an open space in the factory and gave them a long lecture. Roxi only understood the first sentence. She couldn't listen to the rest of his words. The death of the factory was like a heavy burden of sadness in her heart. She wondered why nobody cried. On the contrary, everybody was silent and indifferent. Even Mr. Smith said something (was it something funny?), and the sound of laughter filled the space around her. Roxi was even more surprised. Maybe this is their custom, she thought. Even in death they laugh and make fun. She remembered the sitcoms on TV. Laughter was heard every once in awhile for no good reason. She wondered why she was thinking of such things. When she saw everybody walking in one direction, she didn't know what to do. Natasha took hold of her arm and pulled her.

"Where?" she asked.

"Farewell party."

"A party?"

No, she couldn't go to any party.

She wanted to sit in a corner and cry. Then she realized that she didn't have to stand behind the machine and label bottles anymore. A breath that had stayed captured inside her for six years and five months was released. She remembered her beautiful park. That morning she had passed by it, and it had left a magnificent and richly splendid memory.

She took off her uniform, put her lay-off letter in her purse and got out of the factory. The atmosphere in the factory, the silent machines resembled dead corpses about to decay. They smelled stale and bitter.

She waited for the bus, which was less frequent at this time of day. The blue sky was like an umbrella above her head. A cold feeling was sitting inside her, right underneath her heart. From that moment she knew that her bond with the factory was broken, she had felt it there. Many times she had squeezed it. A morbid thought passed through her mind: What if she had a heart attack? She took many deep breaths, she noticed the bus coming from far off. She smiled at the thought of going to the park. The coldness beneath her heart didn't lessen. The bus reached the stop and a few people got off and on. Roxi sat on a seat and the bus started. Roxi's thoughts were far away. She stared outside. She saw a woman in front of her, right behind the driver. She couldn't remember where the woman had got on the bus. First she couldn't trust her own eyes. She blinked many times. Maybe what she was seeing was only her imagination. But it wasn't. It was a woman exactly the same as she was: the same height and the same figure, as if she was seeing her own image in the mirror. She wanted to get up and touch her, but she didn't dare. The bus reached the park. The woman descended, and Roxi, too, involuntarily got off the bus. The woman sat on a bench under the trees, Roxi followed her and sat beside her. Many times she opened her mouth to talk to her, but words wouldn't come.

The woman was as silent as a tomb, and she was looking off into space. A book was in her hands, the same one that Roxi was reading, by a young writer.

In the silence of that spring morning, the park, the trees and the open spaces between the trees were all deep in thought. It was an unusually windless day for this windy city. Roxi felt sleepy. She had the desire to lie down for a much-needed sleep. For six years and five months and three days she had woken up every morning, like a mechanical toy, at the same hour. In the twilight hours of the morning, she had prepared breakfast for Peimaan, made his sandwich, even sometimes cooked the dinner. Nader would still be in bed all this time. For the past three out of four years, she hadn't seen much of Nader either. When she did, he was still sleeping. And once in a while at parties in their friends' homes, or in their own home when their friends were over, or once a year at Nowruz for a few hours. The pizza business used up all of Nader and all that he had left for home was sleep.

Roxi thought, not thinking; since she had seen her twin (she had given her this name), she was not able to think anymore. Thoughts were becoming lighter and lighter in a mass of condensed clouds in her head. The only thought she had in her head was that she wanted to lie down under the trees. Although she had her own home, an apartment on the twenty-fifth floor of a thirty-six-floor building beside a major highway where vehicles passed incessantly like a roaring river, Roxi had no desire to return home. Her home was empty now, every moment of the day and night. Thinking of this made her sad, as if she were thinking of someone who had died and this made her heart cold again. At the point when the desire to sleep became stronger, she got up. She saw that her twin was walking a little ahead of her. The woman lay down under a tree and put the book and her purse under her head. Then she went to sleep. Roxi thought:

I've messed up.

She didn't feel like sleeping anymore. She only wanted to know how long the woman would sleep there. She wanted to wait for her to wake up, so they could start talking about themselves.

At that moment, she remembered that her real name was Reyhaneh, but she had forgotten that name. She believed that she had become Roxi. Yes, she wanted to talk to the woman. She hadn't talked to anybody for a long time. And now that she had the sadness and death of somebody on her mind she wanted to talk about it. So she waited. Little by little she felt the colour of happiness in her heart, the happiness of release. The happiness of being drowned in the green that surrounded her, the sky as blue as a child's memory and the birds whose songs were not bothering the silence of the trees. At the same time, she was uncomfortable with this happiness. One should not be happy at the death of a loved one. Roxi would be happy for her twin to wake up. She sat there. She didn't know for how long. She saw that spring changed to summer and summer changed to fall. The leaves on the trees became yellow, then orange, and red. They fell from the trees and Roxi's twin was still asleep under the tree. Maybe she had gone to her eternal sleep. Roxi only came to herself to realize that the woman had been covered with dried leaves. Then she got up and went home.

Her home was silent, not unlike any other day when she got home from the factory at six o'clock. Nader was busy in his pizzeria, cooking and delivering pizzas. Peimaan, in another city, was wrestling with his studies. She cooked for herself. She watched TV. She had to laugh at sitcoms that were not even funny. Watch the advertising for the hundredth and thousandth times and curse it. Then she took a nap, and read the Iranian newspapers, called a few friends and had the same conversation. And then it was time to sleep. Close to dawn, she would feel Nader's presence, sometimes his body smelled of sex. She would get up, go to Peimaan's room that was empty now, sleep in his bed. She could still smell that smell in her sleep. She wanted to throw up, she would have a nightmare, she would dream of George making love with Natasha, she would dream Natasha's husband had come to their place looking for an Iranian girl. She would wake up. Remembering Iran, she thought hard but couldn't remember the name of the street where her cousin Nastaran lived. She would go back to sleep and dream about the automatic machine being set up in their living room. She was scared of it. Nader was working with it. He wanted to make pizza with it. She would get up with the alarm clock and leave for the factory without breakfast.

She took a deep breath. It was wonderful that she didn't have to go back to work the next day. Then the sadness of losing a loved one captured her soul again. She didn't cry. She called Nader and gave him the news of the factory being shut down.

"What about the automatic machine?" he asked. "Didn't they order it?"

"I don't know."

"So you were only torturing me and yourself by imagining it?"

"That wasn't my fault."

She hung up. Her life was strangely empty now. The one who had died had left Roxi with empty days and nights. She lay down on the sofa, remembering her twin.

She was lucky, she was very brave, she thought. She tried not to think about the future. But the future was like the automatic machine. It was there and it wasn't there. It was supposed to come. It was coming and not coming. Eleven years, seven months and eight days passed. Then Roxi became Reyhaneh again and she forgot the name Roxi. She passed away in a hospital in this city. Her husband, her son and her daughter-in-law, who after six years of marriage still didn't want to get pregnant, were with her. They couldn't have known what was happening inside her.

Occasionally they saw a smile on her face. Sometimes she would reach out a hand for something. Reyhaneh was still in her beautiful park. The same park that she had passed by for six years, five months and three days. And every day she had wished that she could spend an hour among its trees and listen to the song of birds. Reyhaneh was lying down under the trees on the green grass, was waiting for the trees to change colour and pour down their leaves in a gentle breeze. Reyhaneh saw her twin, she smiled at her and said hello. She was greeted back.

"Father, Reyhaneh is saying hello," Peimaan said.

"To whom? To me?" Nader asked.

The twin said, "Not to you. To me."

This story is written in memory of Ghazaleh Alizadeh, an Iranian writer who committed suicide by hanging herself from a tree in a green area in northern Iran.

The English translation of this story was published in Dandelion, *volume 24, November 1997.*

BLAME

*Y*ES, I SHOULD TELL YOU HOW it began the year we arrived in Canada. It was like a nightmare. It wasn't my choice to uproot my family and come to Toronto. I did not know anything about Toronto. I was living happily in Ahwaz with my wife and two daughters, six and three years old. Ahwaz and Toronto! Just imagine: winter in Ahwaz and winter in Toronto. Not comparable at all. As if you've been taken from a paradise and dropped in a deep-freezer, minus twenty degrees and a wind that could take the skin off your face. For me it wasn't just the weather; there was uprooting and being nobody and nothing without any job or income, which hurt me more than the cold and homesickness. And the most important thing was not knowing the language, which paralyzed me as if I was deaf and dumb. Looking at the innocent faces of Hanieh and Helia, whom I had to disappoint when they wanted me to buy them a little box of chocolate. My wife comforted me with nice words, *It will be okay, don't worry, don't be upset*. That hurt me even more. I became like an incapable person, unable to do anything. Well, I was somebody in my own homeland—head of a department in a big factory.

My wife got a job in a coffee shop and worked from the early evening to five in the morning. She didn't talk about her work and how hard it was. And if she did, what could I do? Once, I went to her workplace and noticed how her employer treated her as if she was her maid. She looked so small behind that counter, even though she is a fairly tall woman. With the cap on her head and wearing a uniform she looked like a stranger to me. She begged me to go home, thinking that I might make a problem for her.

In Ahwaz my wife was a high school teacher—a university graduate in literature. She had a newspaper with her students at school.

Well, do you think we came here of our own will? Or that we had a formal invitation to immigrate here? No, just to reach Turkey we had to go through so much difficulty; we had to drive for more than two days and nights, non-stop with two little kids, and we had to pay lots of money. It was like a nightmare.

Neither my wife nor I was politically active. And we didn't even have passports. We had never needed passports. We didn't have any plans to travel abroad. We weren't rich enough to spend our vacations in Europe or elsewhere outside our country. But as our great poet Shamloo says, we didn't worry for our daily bread and butter and we had a good life more or less.

It is true we went to demonstrations against the shah and sang slogans such as *Death to the shah*. Almost everyone participated in the demonstrations; we did, too. If we hadn't we would have had problems in our workplaces. I was somebody there. Not that I was an engineer or anything like that. No, I was a welding technician. I was an expert in my field; the manager of a big section of the factory and I had a good salary. I had a house of my own with three bedrooms, living room, kitchen and a big yard with a lawn and flower beds.

I was born in Ahwaz, a city in Khuzestan, in the south of Iran. We were nine brothers and sisters. My father was a worker for the oil company. He earned enough to feed us. But he couldn't afford to send all of his children to Tehran to study at the university. Also, being accepted in university wasn't easy, and I was not. But I graduated from the technical school in my birth city. So, after I graduated I got a job at the factory and got married.

In Ahwaz my life was like a flowing stream, and the hot weather wasn't a problem. In fact, I didn't feel it that much. We had air-conditioning at work and at home. Fall and winter were great— mild weather and green everywhere, no snow at all.

Then what happened? War fell over our heads like a nightmare. What could I do? Stay in Ahwaz—a war zone—until my wife and children were killed by Iraqi rockets? No, I didn't have guts for the war. It was on the second night of Iraq's attack that I collected what I could and fled along with my wife and children. It wasn't only me who did that. Anyone who could did the same thing and escaped from the war zones with only a few things—left our homes and all our belongings to be destroyed by the Iraqis' rockets and bombs or be looted by vagabonds. But it was the only logical act for us. If we had stayed and, God forbid, one of us had been killed I would have been sorry for the rest of my life. But what for? And why? And for whom? We haven't had our lives for nothing. How many times do we have a chance to live in this world?

We were able to reach Turkey. I didn't want to go to Tehran, nor any other city in Iran. If I had to be uprooted from my birth city, let it be for a place far away and safe. I was disappointed in our government. They were talking of war as a blessing and saying that it would continue for twenty years.

I didn't want my children killed in the war, so we fled. In a week, we found out that we could seek asylum from the United Nations.

Anyway, it happened quickly, and after a while we were in Toronto in the middle of winter. It snowed for twenty-four hours and everywhere was white, covered with snow, and the weather was so cold that our breath could freeze. But there was no bombardment, no rockets!

From the first week living in Toronto, I had a terrible feeling of homesickness that sometimes paralyzed me.

In winter the weather in Ahwaz was like spring but in Toronto, the bitter cold really tortured me. It wasn't only the weather, but the vast and terrible helplessness that I was feeling froze me to my bones. I could see that my children didn't like their school nor their teachers, whom they couldn't understand. But gradually they started to get to know their environment, made a few Iranian friends and therefore we had some social interaction with their parents and were able to get away from the trap of our solitude.

Our real problems started when the government assistance was cut off. In fact, that assistance hadn't been enough anyway, and even with my wife's job in the coffee shop and me doing pizza delivery some nights when my wife was at home, we still couldn't make ends meet. These were subsistence jobs paying little money, not enough for a family of four.

I asked myself again and again, what had I done that I had to pay such a high price in this world?

My wife didn't say too much about her hardships at work. She always consoled me, saying that we'd be okay. During the day, she took courses to get certificates in typing and bookkeeping and then she was able to get a job in a private company. Her wages weren't much higher than what she got in the coffee shop, but she was happier and said that she was getting experience in a new field. In her resumé, she didn't mention her university degree: otherwise she might have been turned down for being overqualified. Anyway, she continued to take more courses to improve her English, determined to be a teacher in this country as she had been in Ahwaz.

Finally I found a job as well. I prepared a resumé and went from one factory to another. But because of free trade between the U.S., Canada and Mexico, the factories were closing one after the other. And if I had an interview I always heard the same question about my Canadian experience, which made me frustrated.

So, under these circumstances, I had to lower my expectations. I prepared a resumé suitable for a security guard in a high-rise building. In the first interview I thought I was right for the job. There was only me and another guy who was younger and more vigorous than me. The building was located in one of the wealthy neighbourhoods in Toronto. I guessed that the man who did the interview would choose me because of my education and nationality. I was very proud of being Iranian. I showed high self-esteem and bragged about the three thousand years of our history, and our great kings Syrous and Daryous.

The interviewer looked like one of those typical Canadians, with blond hair, and blue eyes and a strong body. He treated me nicely and by chance, he knew Iran, especially Khuzestan. He told me that he had been in Iran twice when he was very young as his father had been working for the Water and Power Authority in Ahwaz. He mentioned Isfahan and Shiraz and talked about Iranians on the street who had welcomed them and treated them with respect and kindness. Even though I couldn't grasp completely what he said about my country, from his smile and his words I realized that he had a good image of Iran and Iranians. He said his father always talked about his time in Iran, saying they were the best years of his life.

He didn't ask too much about my education and my experience. My thought was that he would choose me. He said in a few days he would call me. When I left, I looked at the tall building, which seemed to touch the sky, and imagined it had been built or bought by the money his father had earned in Iran.

That night I went home with a box of pastry, even though I had a feeling of being put down. People who worked in Iran and got the best salaries and attention, as he had described, were accepted and welcomed wherever they went, and now they had the upper hand in decisions about our future. And we had to bring ourselves low to get a job and work like a slave.

A week later I was called for the second interview. My wife and I were sure that the job was mine. I went to the place with joy and hope, then had to wait in the hallway for more than one hour. When I went in, it wasn't the same person but the manager of a big company. I stretched my hand to shake his and he did it, but with reluctance. I sat down without waiting for him to tell me. He didn't even look me in the eye.

After a while, which seemed too long to me, he lifted his head and looked at me and asked, "Why did you have a revolution? You had everything during the shah's time." I didn't know how to answer. I wanted to say, *I didn't cause it, and it's because of the revolution I'm here*. But in fact it was my fault, too. I had been in demonstrations. Of course I did it because of the fear of Hezbollah.

Without waiting for me to answer, he continued, "Why did you take the American embassy's employees as hostages?"

I was shocked. I wanted to say, I lived in Ahwaz, and the American embassy was in Tehran, nearly eight hundred kilometres away. But it seemed he considered me a representative of the Iranian government. For half an hour he talked about how ruthless our revolution and the Islamic government were. I was speechless. I wanted to say, I agree, and it's because of that government that I'm here to beg you for a job that is far below what I'm capable of doing.

When he dismissed me, it didn't cross my mind to ask him about the job I was interviewing for. I realized he thought I was responsible for the American hostages in Iran. I just put my head down and went home. But a terrible anger burned inside me, and I didn't know who was I angry with or what was the reason for my anger.

But I didn't talk to anyone about my second interview, not even my wife. If I had had to talk about it, I probably would have cursed and yelled. So I hid my anger. I couldn't justify the man's behaviour. He seemed a stupid, arrogant, and small-minded man who wanted to humiliate me. Not even this conclusion could calm me down. I believed punishing someone who had not been responsible for a crime was also a big crime.

But as folks say, time heals all wounds. A few weeks passed and I sent a resumé for a position as security guard in another building, and I got the job after the second interview.

Our children were busy with their schoolwork and became familiar with the new environment. They didn't have any problem speaking and understanding English.

Winter changed to spring and then it was summer and on some Sundays we went to picnic with friends. Meanwhile I had time during the day to take courses in college related to my qualifications, After four years in this country and those classes, I got a job in my own field, in a factory. The factory was located in Oshawa and I had to drive one hundred kilometres to get there. But I liked the nature of the work and the salary was satisfactory as well.

During this time my wife passed the language exam for the university and registered for a one-year program in a teachers' college, then was hired by the Toronto Board of Education.

Life was much better. We bought a house and two cars. We travelled in summer, we took a trip to Cuba, a place many of our Iranian friends had been to. We travelled to Boston, where my wife's brother lived. And Canada wasn't a bad place anymore. We did not mind the cold. To tell the truth, we didn't feel it very much. Our home, workplace and cars were warm in winter, and spring and summer were magnificent.

Two years passed. I was comfortable with my job at the factory and language wasn't a problem anymore.

One of the night shift security guards retired and the factory had to hire someone to replace him. On the day of the interview the manager called me and said he had an urgent job to attend to and couldn't be there. He asked me to do the interview with the applicant.

When the applicant entered the room, I was reviewing his resumé. I looked up and thought I saw the person who hadn't accepted me as the security guard for his building. I think he recognized me. But I pretended that I didn't recognize him. I thought it might be just a resemblance. But when he started to talk, I remembered all that he had said to me and the arrogant behaviour that had hurt me to my bones. I stared at him for a while. His hair was messy and a lock fell on his forehead. His eyes also weren't so blue but grey and there were some wrinkles around his eyes that showed he had aged. He didn't have a pressed suit on; his dress was casual. Why didn't he acknowledge me? He might also remember how he had hurt me with his prejudice.

For a while I thought I should forget about the past and treat him nicely. My boss had told me whoever I chose would be okay with him.

But I could not forget how this man had treated me, how he had talked to me, which had left me hot with anger and hatred. I asked him a few questions that were not related to the job and sent him away, telling him to wait for a call.

When he left the room, as if I was paralyzed, I could not feel anything. I was not happy or sad. I was mostly angry. Angry with myself and with him. What had happened to the man I thought was manager of a building? Why was he looking for a job as a night shift security guard in this factory? But whatever he had been in that building, why did he treat me like an enemy? Why did he consider me responsible for the American hostages?

But the thing that hurt me more after the interview was my own behaviour.

I was fighting with myself for a week to call him for a second interview, but remembering the first one, I felt ashamed.

Someone else was hired for the position. But for a long time, it was as if I had a painful secret, a feeling of guilt. Finally I couldn't keep it to myself any longer and told my wife about both interviews. When I finished, my wife didn't say a word, but there was blame in her eyes.

THE INTELLECTUALS

For Fereshteh and Behnaz

*T*HAT NIGHT all the family members got together at Baba's invitation. Something like that didn't happen very often. Kayvan had come from Vancouver and I from Kingston. For dinner we had chelo kabab, which Baba had bought from outside.

The table hadn't been cleared yet when Baba began to talk about his decision. During dinner a bitter silence had hung over the family. Even though Baba tried to talk, and as folks say, to warm up our gathering, his words stayed in the air and didn't touch anyone, as if each of us was busy with his or her own thoughts.

I was thinking about the music that I had promised to compose for a short documentary film that my friend had to make for her school project. I didn't have too much time—I had to do it quickly. Kayvan, as usual, was busy with his food and was immersed in his thoughts. He was a second-year film student at the University of British Columbia. When he had said he wanted to study film, he was not encouraged by Baba and Maman. But he didn't care about their advice or their threats that if he wanted to study film they wouldn't send him a penny and he would have to pay for his education himself. He didn't care, and followed a career he was interested in. Maman and Baba said he blew his chance to be someone, especially in this country where all doors were open to him. I mean, as Maman and Baba imagine, the doors that would be open were he to be a doctor or an engineer, a lawyer or a businessman.

THE INTELLECTUALS

My maman and baba are engineers from the University of Tehran, my maman a civil engineer and my baba a chemical engineer. Maman had such a good marks on the entrance exam for the faculty of engineering that she had been able to choose civil engineering, which accepted the students with higher marks; the students with lower marks, like my baba, had no choice but to study chemical engineering. But to be honest, when we were in Iran it was my baba who made the better income. When he graduated from the university he was hired by a chemical production factory; then he established a company and imported the materials the factory needed. When we were in Iran, as my father said, he shovelled up money. After graduation, Maman was hired by the ministry of housing and urban development. She had to take a few years' leave after Kayvan's birth. Then we had to immigrate and in Canada it was obvious that she would never be able to find a job in her field—like many others. My baba couldn't work as an engineer, either, but he found another way to make money: He got a contract with a company to export its product to Iran. But the Canadian company closed after a few years and my father was jobless again, and so he looked for other work. The best job Maman was able to find was caregiver in a seniors' home, and she still has the same job, taking care of old men and women, which has nothing to do with her experience and specialty. She worked for a while in stores but the wage was too low. I don't know how she found this job but she stayed at it. I think the fear of being unemployed was like a black shadow hanging over her head.

I was still in high school when I sensed my parents were getting old. My mother was always tired and sometimes in a bad mood, and so was my father. When we were in Iran, my mother was joyful, humorous, a witty-repartee kind of person. She had a good voice and at our family gatherings she usually sang songs. Here, she rarely sang. When we were in Iran, she always sang at home and especially when we travelled by car. Maman knew all the songs of lots of different singers by heart. My baba liked my maman's voice. We heard him many times saying, "When I heard her voice for the first time, I fell in love with her." These kinds of comments were from many years ago, when we were in Iran. Since we left there, there had been no talk of love. There was always a bleak atmosphere hanging over our family, mostly because we didn't feel safe and stable in this country. I didn't know whether it was because of our parents' jobs or something else.

That night when my baba talked about his decision, I found out that there was a reason for that the cold ambience.

When we were in Iran, my baba used to call Maman an intellectual. She read books, and whenever she did, she told us the story, too. My maman had a special place in our family. In exile, too, she had her place for a while. I mean, I never noticed that my father insulted her, even though he was the one who had the last word. They didn't argue in front of us; they always respected each other. Here, too, once in a while my father used the word "intellectual" about my mother but she got angry and responded, "You're the intellectual now, not me. You know better than me how to live in this country." One day Kayvan joked, saying, "Be reasonable. Both of you are intellectuals. Don't fight each other." After that Kayvan and I sometimes called them "the intellectuals," and whenever we wanted to tease them we asked, "How are the intellectuals feeling?"

In fact I was always happy with my parents' relationship. At least they didn't end up separating in this country like many other Iranian couples. I didn't notice when their relationship became cold. I imagine it happened when Kayvan and I were away from home.

Once I asked Maman, "Do you regret immigrating?" She shook her head and said, "No. Here I learned a lot."

I think she wasn't telling me the truth. She probably said that because she did not want to disappoint me. What did she learn here? In my opinion my mother had lost her place in society.

So, that night, when the whole family was together, Baba cleared his throat and said, "Your Maman and I have decided to separate. Tomorrow I'll leave the house and put it up for sale. Your mother can live here until it is sold. Then she can have her share and she can do whatever she wants to do."

Maman looked shocked, as if she didn't expect to hear such news. I was very surprised. I expected anything from Baba except this, especially at this time when my mother had just heard that her mother had passed away and she couldn't go to Iran. She reasoned that going was useless after her mother was dead. "I should have gone earlier," she said. During the last ten years of living in Canada, my mother had gone back to Iran just once. Kayvan and I went with her, too. After that first visit she stopped going. She used to say, "Going is good, but returning is not." I remember when we came back from the visit, she talked about Iran nonstop and looked at the pictures she had taken there over and over. Then she put the pictures aside and whenever there was some news about Iran or a family member called her from there, she would say, "I have no place there."

While Baba talked about his decision, Maman said nothing. It was clear that she knew what was going on. Ignoring Baba's words, she got up to clear the table but Baba admonished her, saying to sit down. Maman sat down again and Baba said, "I haven't taken this decision lightly. It has been a while that I feel your maman has no interest in me. Recently she has moved into a separate bedroom."

Maman interrupted him and said, "When?'"

Baba said, "You know better than me. Don't make me say more."

Baba said more but I don't remember what. Then he looked at Kayvan and me and asked, "What do you think?"

Kayvan got up and went to his room and I didn't see him after that. The next morning, Maman said Kayvan had left the house the same night.

I wanted to leave the house, too, but I felt pity for Maman and wanted to know what she was going to do. In fact, she couldn't do anything. It was all Baba's decision.

The next week, when I came home from school, Maman wasn't there. Baba said, "Your mother has left the house and I don't have any news from her."

"Why didn't you call me?"

"I didn't want to worry you, when you had exams."

"You mean my exams are more important than Maman's life?"

"Don't worry. Through Ms. Sarmadi, I mean Ms. Farkhondeh, I found out she's in a shelter. She is in a safe place."

"Which shelter?"

"How should I know? Ms. Farkhondeh Sarmadi knows about her. You know her, that stout woman who made life so hard for her husband who died when he wasn't fifty yet. The one who makes decisions about anyone."

I found Maman's address and went to see her. Her eyes filled with tears but she was able to control herself. I hadn't expected to see her in such a place.

She said, "They didn't want to accept me. They said, 'You haven't been assaulted by your husband. This is a place for women who are assaulted and beaten by their husbands.' I had to tell them that my husband abused me verbally."

"Did he?"

She didn't answer me. I looked at her, and she said, "You saw how he treated me. He was always jealous of me, because I was among the best students at the university and he was not so good. He considered himself inferior to me, but none of this was important to me. Otherwise I would not have married him."

"But he always admired you, and also he earned more money than you."

"Yes, but all were fake gestures. Even here he envied my job. He had to change his job several times."

I looked around and was surprised at how Maman bore the situation.

I said, "When Baba sells the house and gives you your share, buy an apartment for yourself."

"I don't need your father's money."

"It's your money, too."

"No, I spent my income on our daily living expenses such as groceries. He paid for the mortgage."

"If you didn't spend your money on the necessities, he wouldn't have been able to pay the mortgage."

"Don't talk about money. Your father's desire is money, not mine."

"What is your desire, then?"

She looked at me and said nothing, as if she expected me to know the answer.

When I was leaving, I told her I'd be busy for a few months, then I would have to look for a job. "I may not be able to come and see you. You'd better go back to your home. Don't forget that it's your house, too."

"It was. I thought it was."

Then when I said goodbye to her, she said, "Don't worry about me. I'm comfortable here. I am on the list to get subsidized housing. Don't worry about me at all."

I got her telephone number in order to keep in touch with her. But I didn't call. I felt humiliated by her action. I believed that she should have stayed in our family house and got her share. Why didn't she? The way she behaved wasn't clear to me. I was angrier with my mother than with my father. I believed Baba had been truthful with himself, with Maman and with us. He might have reached the point where he believed Maman didn't love him anymore or he didn't love Maman. He had the right to decide about his life. But why did Maman ignore her rights and consider herself an abused woman, while the shelter workers believed she was taking a place away from someone who was really abused.

For two or three months I didn't have any news from my mother. She didn't call me either. It seemed she had cut off herself from all of us. Perhaps it was better this way. I probably didn't know my mother very well. I always thought she put too much energy into making a comfortable life for us. For example, if I asked for a special food, she would prepare it the next day. She sometimes got up early in the morning and made us fresh food to take to school. She was a devoted mother and now it was about three months that she did not want to have news from us. I was angry with her and didn't want to ask about her.

During this period, I went to our house a few times. I always called before going. When I got there, Baba had cleaned up. At least this was my perception. He mostly ordered chelo kabab, which I liked, and in Kingston there weren't any chelo kababi restaurants, and even if there were, I couldn't afford to buy there with my student budget.

My baba always asked me about Maman and when I said I didn't have any news from her, I could see he was happy. He paid more attention to me and was nicer. He believed I had rejected my mother and he liked this.

Once when I went to our house without calling in advance, there was a woman there who introduced herself as Lisa. Baba wasn't home. Lisa said, "He'll be home in an hour." At first I thought she was a cleaner but her easygoing manner showed that she lived there. She offered me tea. She said a few words in Farsi and when Baba came home, he kissed her as if she was his wife and called her "My dear."

That night when I went to my room to sleep, Baba knocked at my door and entered. He sat on the edge of my bed and said, "Lisa and I are going to marry and live in this house."

I asked, "What about Maman's share?"

To tell the truth, I was still angry with Maman but I preferred the house be sold rather than a strange woman be living there instead of my mother.

He said, "Finally I was able to contact your mother and talk to her about selling the house. She said, 'You can do whatever you like. Take my share, too.' Your mother is a stubborn woman. And if she insists on ignoring her share, I might as well keep it for myself. So, I have decided to marry Lisa, and then half of this house will be Lisa's, not your mother's."

I said nothing. As my mother used to say, *You can't help someone else take action*. She wanted it this way.

I decided to go back to Kingston the next day and forget about having a mother and father, but somehow I found myself in the shelter asking about my mother. They said she had got a place and left the shelter. When they realized I was her daughter, they gave me her address and her telephone number. I called and told her I was coming. An hour later I was there with a bouquet of flowers. At the door, I heard someone playing setar inside. I thought maybe my mother also had a boyfriend who played setar. But when she opened the door, there was no one except her. And a setar was on the table. I asked, "Were you playing setar?" She smiled and said, "Yes. Is there any problem?"

My mother had told me that she had always wished to learn to play an instrument. When she was in elementary and high school, she asked her parents to send her to the music school but they refused. When she finished her education, she said, she bought a setar with her first paycheque as an engineer. But after getting married and having children, there was no time to learn to play. In exile, too, with so many problems, learning music was out of the question.

With a smile she continued, "Now it's the best time for me to learn an instrument. My fingers aren't quick but it keeps me occupied. Sometimes I practise for a few hours, unaware of how time passes."

It's a few years now since my parents separated and each of them has their own life. My father married Lisa as soon as he was divorced from my mother. And a year later they had a son.

For a while I thought my father was a winner in this separation and happier: he had the house and a younger wife, who helps him in his work in his real estate office, plus he had a son and he would probably be able to make him into an engineer or a doctor. But my mother got nothing. When I asked her why she wasn't looking for a companion, in order not to be so lonely, she said, "I'm not lonely." She was right. Whenever I went to see her, I could hear her playing the setar, or singing a song, or reading a book. There was some kind of satisfaction in her face but sometimes a sadness, too.

If I asked her why she was sad, she would say, "I'm not sad." I don't know if she was being honest or not but her satisfaction made me happy.

When I go to my father's house, I see something else. Even though he tries to be happy in my presence, there is a hidden anger in his behaviour and in his words. He screams at Douglas, his son, without any reason. I think my father doesn't like his name. Lisa calls him Doug—it is her father's name and that is why she chose it.

Finally I got my master's degree, but I don't like working in this field. Listening to other people's problems makes me depressed. I also studied music and now I'm studying composition. I was more interested in this subject but because of my parents I studied psychology. Kayvan, too, finished his education and then he went to the U.S. with the hope that one day he would be someone in Hollywood.

THE SPRING SNOWSTORM

All migrants leave their past behind
Although some try to pack it into bundles and boxes
—Salman Rushdie, *Shame*

*H*E CAME TO MY HOME two days after Siamak's funeral. He had called me before coming and said, "You don't know me, but Siamak did. We were on the same path for a short time, a very short time …"

He paused for a while and then continued, "Hearing of his death or …" And then he paused again for while before going on: "I'm really sorry. I didn't want to …"

He didn't use the word "suicide." It seemed to me he was trying not to cry. I didn't know what to say. Who was this person I'd never heard of? He said, "I'd like to come see you." He said, "I was at Siamak's funeral but I didn't expect you to notice me. Perhaps there were many people you didn't know, who might have been Siamak's patients. I thought if I met you I would be able to …"

Again, he didn't finish his sentence.

We arranged that the next day he would come to my house. When he arrived, I still didn't recognize him.

He said he had recently come from Iran to visit his brother, who had brain cancer, and the doctors had given up on his treatment.

I was waiting for him to tell me how he knew Siamak. I remembered his words on the phone: *We were on the same path for a short time*. I was waiting for him to talk, but it seemed it was hard for him to carry on. He seemed disturbed. Now and then he looked around the room and gazed out the window. The magnificent Toronto autumn made a beautiful scene outside. His eyes stopped on one of my paintings, which he said resembled the scenery. I had painted it from the place where he had sat down. It wasn't just him who said that. Everyone who had seen the painting in autumn had the same idea. I started painting about seven or eight years ago and spent several hours per day painting scenery and landscapes. He then looked at me, as if he had a question he couldn't verbalize. The atmosphere was heavy. To break the silence, I said, "I painted it."

He said, "I thought Siamak did."

Siamak was interested in all kinds of arts and admired all artists. He read books more than anyone I know. His special interest was novels and he used to say a good novel is like a psychiatrist, analyzing the minds of human beings.

The silence was heavy. I don't know why I didn't ask him how and where he met Siamak and how far back their friendship went. I imagined it might have been a friendship between them because he called him Siamak, and not Dr. or Mr. Parsapoor.

It was more than a week since Siamak had died and I couldn't believe it yet. I felt his absence in every place and in every moment of my life and I talked to him in my head. Death was believable, but not suicide. If Siamak had been a young man, if he had had some problems and "ifs," I could have justified his suicide, but there was no reason for it. I heard from other people that Iranian society was shocked by Siamak's suicide and I was even more so.

To initiate talking to this man, I said, "Excuse me," as if I did not know how to treat a guest, and after a pause, I asked, "Coffee or tea or a cold drink?" He looked at me and said, "I don't want to bother you."

I said, "Please, it's not bothering."

He said, "A coffee if you are having one."

I went to the kitchen and came back with two cups of coffee with milk and sugar, put it in front of him and sat down. The coffee could help to break the silence. When there's a lull in the conversation, a drink can help break the silence. He sipped his coffee, and stared at the tree outside the window, which was still covered with coloured leaves, and then his eyes wandered around the room and said, "You have a beautiful house."

And he waited for me to reply, but I just smiled and said nothing. I was still wondering why this stranger had come to my house.

I asked him, "How did you know Siamak?"

He said, "I didn't know him very well. We were supposed to travel together but it didn't happen, and we didn't see each other after that."

I wondered what to say.

And after a short pause, he continued, "And now I think Siamak's suicide could have a connection with my visit."

I said, "Did you see him again?"

"Yes."

"When?"

"One day before his suicide."

A feeling of fear and anxiety crawled under my skin. My coffee became bitter in my mouth. I put the cup on the table. The man was a death messenger. My tongue was frozen in my mouth. Had he come to make me commit suicide, too? What did he want from me?

He said, "Don't panic. I'm not a death messenger. Even though I might have been one for your husband, but this is just a guess. Siamak might have left a note and explained his reason for suicide. In the past week I heard a lot about your husband. He was a well-known person with a good reputation in his field and had done lots of charity work. But why did he suddenly commit suicide? I think there wasn't any reason except meeting me after so many years."

And after a short pause, he continued, "Excuse me if I use his first name. He introduced himself to me with this name and it stayed with me."

I said formally, "As you like." But in fact I was getting impatient. His words were confusing. I couldn't find a clue to what he was talking about and I was getting disturbed, as if I was thinking about something that had nothing to do with death or Siamak's suicide. I was thinking about our mutual past; the years we were new in Canada. Siamak came first. Then he arranged for me and the children to come. We left Iran with our Iranian passports and went to Spain. But from Spain to Canada we had to travel with our fake passports. For a few years we didn't have a comfortable life. Siamak did not have a medical license in Canada and had to work any job to make ends meet. And sometimes he became depressed and had nightmares. I could understand the reason for his depression—it was our unsettled life. A few years later he was able to find a job in a hospital; then his depression was less, even though he still had it once in a while, but as time went by the intervals between his nightmares were longer and his depression was gone.

And these memories were fading in my mind and there was no reason to talk about them. Our refugee claimant status was replaced by "landed immigrant" and then we got our citizenship. Siamak got his psychiatric specialty. Our children, Ardalan and Ida, finished their education and lived their own lives in other cities. Me too: I was busy with my painting, friends and socializing, going to concerts and the theatre. Every other year I travelled to Iran and visited my relatives. There wasn't any reason to complain. But Siamak never returned to Iran. Even though he could have gotten his Iranian passport like many other Iranian refugees, who did, and then travelled back to Iran, he didn't. I was sure he loved Iran and whenever I was going to travel there, he asked me to take pictures. Then when I came back, the first thing he asked me was about the photos. He would look at them for hours and if he had ever been in a particular city or place, he talked about his memories. Sometimes when he wanted to talk about Iran, he got really emotional.

My mind was wandering with these thoughts when the man said, "It seems Siamak didn't have a bad life."

I concentrated again and said, "What do you mean? A specialist would have a good life in any part of the world. After a long time studying and working hard he deserved to have a prosperous life."

He said, "Yes, he deserved it."

But his eyes and his tone didn't say the same thing, as if he was mocking me. His behaviour and his presence were becoming a burden. Who was this person and what did he want from me? I had this question in my mind but it didn't come to my mouth. I was sitting there, perplexed, sometimes lost in the past and sometimes in the present, waiting for him to talk. I really didn't know if he had a clue to Siamak's suicide. Since he had said Siamak's suicide might have a connection with his visit, I was disturbed, but I did not ask any questions, as if I was mesmerized or someone had told me to be patient.

I finally asked the question that had been on my mind all this time: "How did you know Siamak? And why did you come to see him?"

"I told you, Siamak and I were together just for one night."

And I said, "A crucial night?"

"What do you mean? Did he talk about it with you?"

"About what?"

"About our visit, about that crucial night?"

"I don't remember."

In fact, Siamak had told me something about it, but honestly, I wasn't in a mood to repeat what Siamak had told me. I was waiting for this man to tell me the story of that night, as he called it a crucial night.

He said, "It's strange."

"Why strange?"

"Forget it. What do you think? Do you think Siamak's suicide is related to my visit?"

"You said so."

"You should know better than me. You were partners."

"Siamak didn't have any problem as far as I know."

"Was there another woman?"

"Even if there was, there's no reason that I would talk about it with you."

"You're right. I'm a stranger, but I really want to know the reason behind Siamak's suicide. Then I wouldn't feel guilty. To tell the truth, since Siamak killed himself after my visit, I have called myself a death messenger. Now you're talking to a death messenger."

I thought he was speaking nonsense. I asked him, "Why do you call yourself that? Did you kill Siamak?"

He mumbled, "You know very well that I didn't. He killed himself and you are his partner but you don't know the reason, or you maybe know it and don't want to tell me."

With anger in my voice I said, "And now you're here to find out about the reason for Siamak's suicide, or you know about it and don't want—"

He interrupted me and said, "Don't take this the wrong way. I'm really sorry about Siamak's suicide. I've been guilty for two deaths—two accidental deaths, and not suicide."

I think he noticed I was panicking and said, "Don't panic. I'm not a murderer. If I was, I wouldn't be sitting in front of you." And he continued, "Everything happened on that night when I met Siamak."

After a relatively long silence I sighed and said, "Tell me about that night, the night you met him. That night was significant in Siamak's life."

"So, you know something."

Siamak had told me that the night he was fleeing the country through the mountains, a young couple with a two- or three-months-old baby were supposed to be with him. In fact, when the smuggler found out that Siamak was a physician, he asked him to accompany the couple, and told him that their baby was sick. When Siamak asked why he was sending a young couple with a sick baby on such a difficult journey, the smuggler said they didn't have any other choice and it was their own will to leave the country. Siamak and the couple set out on the journey and they were supposed to follow each other. But before they'd gone a long way a snowstorm started. The man, who was very young, saw the deep valleys beside them, and stopped, not wanting to continue. He said he didn't want to risk his family's life and he and his wife and child turned around and went back. But Siamak continued the trip and, before sunrise, crossed the border.

That was all Siamak had told me and unwillingly I told the man this.

He asked, "And what about that family?"

"Which family?"

"That young man, his wife and the baby?"

"How do I know what happened to them? Siamak said the man decided to go back. He said the man changed his mind. He might have found another way to flee the country."

He stared at me for a while, and to tell the truth, I was scared. What did he have in his mind?

I said, "Now tell me, are you the same man?"

"Yes, I am."

And he didn't say anything. His silence was long and scary.

I said, "Well, tell me."

"I'm thinking whether to tell you or not."

"Are you worried that I will kill myself?"

"People's reactions are unpredictable."

I was very mad. "Why don't you talk clearly?"

"Truthfully, I regret coming here."

Angrily, I said, "Why did you then?"

He stared at me for a while and then said, "I made a mistake."

I looked at him. He had made me so furious that my body was burning. What had he said to Siamak that made him commit suicide? Was he right that he had been with Siamak for only one night? And now after so many years he had come back to take his life?

He realized that I was disturbed. I burst into tears and instead of talking to him, curses poured out of my mouth. The man was panicky. He got up and went to the kitchen, brought me a glass of water and said, "I didn't mean to hurt you." He said he was very sorry for Saimak's death.

I screamed, "Please leave me alone," and almost told him to get out. But the man was really apologetic. I was in control again, after drinking some water.

I said, "I wish you to tell me the truth. You're just talking ambiguously."

He said, "Believe me, I regret coming here and am even more regretful for visiting Siamak. I didn't think that—"

I said, "So, whatever happened is because of what you told him."

"I'm afraid so."

I said angrily, "Now what do you want from me? You have come here to tell me that Siamak's hands are smeared with the blood of a few people? Or he beheaded your wife and your child and fled away?"

He said nothing. His silence was annoying. Siamak had told me many times that he would like to have known what happened to that young couple and their baby, but he didn't know how to find out.

When for the first time I was able to get my Iranian passport and was going to Iran, to visit my parents, I remembered his dangerous trip and told him, *If you like, I'll try to find that family and talk to them. Their baby must be an adult by now.*

Siamak had pondered for a while and then said, "I don't remember his or her name. And I'm not sure if he had told me his real name. Don't bother. I'm sure they have forgotten about me."

But all these years, whenever he remembered that treacherous night and that young couple, a dark shadow sat on his face. I used to tell him, it is not possible that you can find out about all those who fled Iran. He probably did go back, or found another way to flee.

And Siamak would say bitterly, "Or he might have been captured by guards ..."

And now that man was sitting in front of me, and I didn't want to know the story of what happened to them on the mountain with their sick baby in the snowstorm.

The man was quiet and suddenly got up and said he'd better go.

"I don't understand why you came to my home?"

"Just to offer condolences, and also I wanted to know the reason for Siamak's suicide, but unfortunately you won't tell me."

With anger I said, "As I don't know, how can I tell you? But it seems that you know, and I wonder why you don't want to tell me. You've raised a doubt in me, a suspicion that Siamak has committed an unforgivable sin."

He replied, "If you think this way, then I'll tell you my story. Siamak also wanted to know. In fact, I didn't want to tell him about that night but he wanted to know."

"Well, if you've told him, tell me, too. I won't kill myself, since I wasn't there that night."

He sat down again and continued, "When the smuggler found out that Siamak was a doctor, he asked him to accompany us and he accepted and said he would be happy if he could help. Less than an hour after we started our walk, a snowstorm began. I got worried for my wife and baby. We reached a shelter. It was Siamak's suggestion that we enter the shelter and wait for the snowstorm to finish. Siamak said the spring storms in the mountain don't last for long. Once in a while he went out from the shelter to see if the storm was over and all the time he kept talking to my wife and me, saying we would cross the border before the dawn. But when Siamak left for the last time to check the weather, he didn't come back. I went out. The snowstorm was not so strong but there was no sign of Siamak. To tell the truth, I didn't dare to call his name in the mountains in that dark night. I thought there were guards in those areas, though it might have been my imagination. A person who is fleeing is afraid of his own shadow. Eventually I gave up hope of Siamak's return. I thought he had lost his way or had fallen off the cliff into one of those deep valleys. I decided not to carry on with our plan."

I asked him, "Did you go back?"

"I did. But not with my wife and my child."

"What do you mean?"

It was like someone else was talking. He said, "I returned to the shelter and told my wife, 'I don't dare continue.' My wife agreed. So we decided to go back. We had no knowledge of the route and the snowstorm was unpredictable. There were deep valleys. I was worried my wife couldn't make it, especially because my child was sick. I was worried the baby would freeze in the middle of the night. Thinking about Siamak, who might have lost his life because of us, upset me. I started to go back with my wife. The snowstorm became heavy again and walking was more difficult. In a moment my wife's feet slid and before I could get hold of her, she fell into a deep valley with her baby held tightly to her chest. Now you can guess what I had to endure."

I interrupted him and asked, "Did you tell everything to Siamak?"

"I didn't want to, but he insisted on knowing. He wanted to know all the details and then I told him. Now I think that was the reason for Siamak's suicide. I'm really sorry. Believe me, if I was as brave as Siamak, I should have killed myself, too. But I am not as brave and I wasn't on that night, either. So he was a winner and I am a loser."

And I was left wondering: Was Siamak a winner or a loser?

LET'S READ ULYSSES

HAIDEH HAD A SIP OF HER COFFEE, put the mug on the table and looked at Satar, who'd just arrived. She asked him, "What about Nazanin? Why isn't she with you?"

Satar was staring at a newspaper on the table. Then he sat down, looked at Haideh and absent-mindedly said, "She had a headache, one of those severe headaches that once in a while hit her and make her miserable. Her job is nerve-racking and her headaches ..."

Without paying any more attention to Satar, Haideh brought her cup to her lips. To the group, Nazanin's headaches and her absence weren't a new subject.

Satar said, "Well, I've promised Nazanin to be at home at eight. Her brother is here from Montreal for a few days."

Haideh said, "Weren't we supposed to have one night per month for ourselves?"

"Tonight is an exception," Satar said.

Azad was daydreaming. Then he looked around. There were a few young people in the coffee shop and all of them were busy with their laptops, iPads or iPhones. A middle-aged couple was sitting at a farther table, talking in a language that sounded strange to Azad. "Someone Like You," an Adele song, was playing.

Azad was distracted by Adele's voice. Haideh put her hand on his shoulder and said, "You're again lost in your own world. Why don't you say anything?"

Azad came back to his senses and said, "Have you already started?"

Haideh said, "Where are you?"

The song was finished.

Haideh said, "Wake up."

Satar said, "We should start."

Farzin said, "Yes, we'd better start." He looked at his watch and continued, "Time flies. We haven't started yet and half an hour is gone."

Haideh said, "Because Satar was late for part of it."

Satar said, "Well, make it quick. I told you, I have to leave early. Now, do you want to start or not?"

Azad said, "For sure we want to start. Otherwise why are we here?"

Haideh put her hand on Azad's shoulder and said, "Don't complain. You'd better start. You've read the story?"

Azad said, "Yes, I read it. Shouldn't I?"

Together, Farzin and Haideh said, "How was it?"

Azad put the empty mug on the table and said, "It wasn't bad. It has a strong structure; for a novice writer, it was a good story."

Farzin interrupted Azad. "She's not a novice. She's published two collections of short stories and a novel."

Azad said, "For me she was a novice."

Haideh asked, "Don't you have something more to say?"

Azad said, "Like what?"

Farzin said, "Criticizing the story."

Azad said, "What do you mean by 'criticizing'?"

Haideh said, "He means, tell us your point of view. Was it a good story or not?"

Azad said, "Why don't you talk about it? We discussed it last night."

Haideh said, "Last night? Last night we didn't talk about this story."

"So, which story did we talk about?"

"We talked about another story by another writer."

Azad said, "Whatever. You talk about it."

Farzin looked at Haideh and said, "Yes, you tell us about it."

Haideh said, "In my view, it was a good story. It was eloquent.

The writer lives in Iran and knows the language very well. She's not like us, following through the newspapers and Iranian sites and the radio."

Azad said, "Don't make it too long. Don't be philosophical. Tell us your main point of view."

Haideh said, "Again, you're nagging. Here is not like our home, where you don't let me talk.

Farzin said, "It's better to leave your argument at home. Haideh was talking about her point of view—she was talking about the language of the story. Haideh always notices some points in the stories that none of the rest of us see. She mostly looks at the characters rather than the style and technique."

Haideh said, "He's right. For me the characters are more important."

So far Satar had been quiet, as if he was busy with his own thoughts rather than listening to the group. He came to his senses now and said, "Can you tell me the difference between 'story' and 'tale'?"

Haideh said, "You tell us. Your knowledge of literature is much wider than ours. I mean, myself; I mean, you've studied literature."

Satar said, "Don't rely on me. Once I taught literature at the University of Tehran, but not anymore. None of us are the same people as we were in our country."

Farzin said, "Me too—I used to be an engineer and signed big contractors."

Haideh said, "Men and their big egos. Me too, I was a housewife and had nothing to do except to care for my children. And now ..."

Azad said, "Forget it, all of you. We have come here to talk about literature and for a few hours to be—"

Haideh interrupted him and said, "Stop boasting about your past."

Farzin said, "Haideh was going to tell us what she thinks about the story."

Satar said, "Story or tale?"

Haideh said, "Whatever. I mean, whatever you consider it."

Azad said, "Don't mix up the subjects. Tell us your point of view, if you have one, and then I'd like to hear Satar's, which could be interesting."

Satar said, "Please. No compliments. First, I have a question."

Azad, Haideh and Farzin asked together, "What question?"

Satar inquired, "Why did you choose this story?"

Farzin said, "Haideh did. Haideh reads books more than all of us. She looks through most of the Iranian websites and she's more familiar with Iranian literature."

Azad said, "Haideh mostly reads Farsi. I tell her to read English but she doesn't listen to me."

Annoyed, Haideh said, "How many times do I have to tell you, I'm not comfortable reading English. I can't understand the language very well."

Farzin said, "I can't believe you. You speak English as fluently as a nightingale."

Haideh said, "My English is good enough to talk at the level of kindergarten children. I don't have any problem talking to them."

With a smile, Satar said, "Does a nightingale speak English?"

Haideh let loose one of those loud laughs and said, "Does a nightingale speak? Farsi or English or whatever?"

Azad said, "It seems that tonight Haideh and Satar have decided to make it exciting. I don't think Satar has read the story or the tale. And it seems that Haideh doesn't have anything to say about it."

He looked at Haideh and said, "Well, my dear, tell us what you have to say."

"You're the one who hijacks the subject all the time." She cleared her throat and said, "I think the story was good. I mean it was intriguing. But ..." And then she stopped.

Farzin said, "Why don't you summarize the story."

Haideh said, "The story is about a woman who devotes her life to her husband and children. She even declines a job promotion because it would mean she would have to travel and stay in the office for longer hours. She wants to be home before her husband and children so that she can prepare food for them and be with them. So her husband doesn't feel that his wife has been working, even though part of the household expenses are covered by her income. When the woman finds out that her husband has taken another wife, lawfully, she just cries in secret. When her daughter and son find out about their father's second wife and realize their mother has accepted the second marriage, they say nothing. But when the son and daughter find out that their mother has been diagnosed with breast cancer and notice that she isn't the lovely and joyful woman she used to be, the son screams at her, telling her that whatever has happened to her is her own fault and the real guilty one is her. He says that she shouldn't have been quiet when her husband married again. She should have left her husband, he says."

Satar said, "I don't know about the story, because I did not read it. But I have a question for Haideh." And after a long pause he said, "Why did you emphasize that the second wife was lawful? Would it have been different if the man had taken the woman as a concubine?"

Haideh said, "Yes, certainly it makes a difference. If they marry legally and then they want to separate, the man has to pay her a dowry, but with a concubine he just needs to recite a verse of the Koran and that's it."

Satar said, "I didn't know that having a concubine was better than marrying."

Farzin said, "Let's not argue about that. You said the story had a problem. What was that?"

Haideh said, "Do you think the son is correct when he screams at his mother and blames her for what his father has done to her?"

Farzin said, "I didn't care about that. The son is angry with his mother because he's losing her. And he can't find a weaker person than her, so he screams at her. But tell us what the problem with the story was."

Haideh said, "Why did the mother not kick her husband out of the house when she found out about his second marriage? She should not have had to leave her own house. She probably had nowhere to go."

And after a while she continued, "Of course one has to be a woman in that country to know the reason."

Satar said, "But this is a short story—fiction, I mean, literature. It's not supposed to solve society's problems."

Haideh said, "But it can draw attention to society's problems. I didn't mean to solve it."

Satar said, "You've learned your lesson very well."

Azad said, "Now it is your turn. What do you think about it?"

Satar looked at them for a while and said, "To tell the truth, I haven't read the story. I mean, I started it but I couldn't finish it." And after a while he continued, "You're like a fisherman who lives by an ocean but every day he goes to a small river to fish. My dear friends, you're living by the ocean of the English culture and literature. Why are you still sticking to that tiny place? Yes, I know the language is a barrier. But all of you have been living here for more than a decade. If you had read just one page a day, do you know how many pages that would have been? You tell me, Farzin, you are an engineer, and know how to calculate. Now multiply three hundred and sixty-five by ten or more. And if you'd learned three or four words each day, by now you would have learned as many words as are in a small dictionary. You could know English much better than James Joyce or Virginia Woolf."

Haideh said, "Why James Joyce and Virginia Woolf? Why did you forget about Shakespeare?"

Azad said, "Shakespeare's works are poetry and plays. We are not reading those genres."

Satar tried to explain his ideas without being offensive. "You're wasting your time, my dears. You've chosen an unknown writer from that devastated …"

Then he paused, took a deep breath and continued, "I mean from your homeland. Stop it. Let's leave that land and its literature to the people who live there. Let's read together James Joyce's works. James Joyce, who wrote *Ulysses*, the novel of the century. And still …"

After a while he went on. "And still many people are wondering how amazing this novel is and—"

Farzin interrupted Satar, which other members of the group didn't dare do.

"What do you mean by 'many people'? You mean us or …"

Satar said, "I mean scholars at the great universities of the world. Yes, they think because they teach literature at prestigious universities and colleges, they are somebody. No, my dear, James Joyce is much greater than all of them."

Then he looked at his watch and said, "Oh my god, it's after eight and I'm still here."

He stood up and as he was putting his coat on said, "Don't waste your time. Swim in the ocean. Remember Forough's poem: *No one will hunt a pearl in a creek streaming in pond.*"

Haideh said, "You've hunted your pearl; now tell us how could we do it?"

Standing, Satar said, "I told you, let's read *Ulysses*."

When Satar left, Haideh, Azad and Farzin looked at each other and for a while they said nothing, as if they were telling each other *Yes, we should swim in the ocean and catch pearls.*

Azad said, "Satar is talking for himself. What's the problem with reading the works of an unknown writer?"

Haideh nodded agreement and added, "Especially when the writer is dealing with a social issue, or shall I say she is dissecting a society's malignant tumour."

Farzin said, "Why has Satar forgotten about so many English-language writers and chosen the biggest pearl in the ocean? Wasn't it possible to choose a less expensive one?"

Azad said, "Well, that's Satar. As he is with us we should benefit from his presence. We can't deny his knowledge. He has a Ph.D. in literature and knows much more than all of us—we are novices about what to read and how to write. I always enjoy his remarks and being with him."

Farzin said, "I admire him as well. I told you to ask Satar to join us. His company is a credit. But don't you think reading *Ulysses* is a bit difficult for us?"

Haideh said, "I'm telling you I'll be drowned the first moment I enter the ocean."

Farzin said, "Let's forget about joking. Let me tell you something. It's up to you to believe it or not, but it's true. I'm part of a writing group in a library. In the past there were more of them and now fewer. I've told you I was in love with literature since I was in high school. I wanted to study literature, but I was accepted in civil engineering and only a fool chooses literature over civil engineering in that country. To keep it short, when I immigrated to Canada, writing again crossed my mind. And because of being nostalgic for my homeland, I started to write."

Haideh interrupted him, "Tell us the truth, was it because of missing Iran or because of Manijeh's leaving you?"

Azad said, "Don't open his wound."

Farzin said, "What can I say about my pain? But when I first was inspired to write, Manijeh was still with me. I mean, she hadn't left me yet."

Then he was quiet.

Azad said, "If Haideh didn't make jokes about everything, it would be better."

Haideh said, "Manijeh's story is over." And she told Farzin, "Please forgive me. Continue your story."

As if Farzin hasn't heard Haideh, he said, "I was going to tell you that I got to know a man, Sean, in one of these workshops I attended. Sean was born and raised in Ireland. He too liked to write. Anyway, we developed a friendship and we saw each other outside the workshop too. In those days I borrowed *Ulysses* from the library, to show that I was interested to read a book from his homeland. But the more I read, the less I understood. I thought I'd better ask my Irish friend, Sean. I told him about my problem and if I tell you what he said, you may not believe me. Yes, he said, I can't understand it either. I remember he talked about the book and said how difficult it is to absorb and fully understand. He said, don't worry if you can't get it. Many people can't, but mostly they pretend they do and show off by repeating James Joyce's name to show their knowledge of literature. I asked him, so why is the book considered the novel of the century? He said, I don't know. There is no doubt that the book is a masterpiece. But me too, I haven't been able to read the book to the end."

Haideh said, "Are you kidding us?"

Azad said, "There's no reason for him to be kidding us."

Haideh said, "What about Satar? You heard what he said—let's read *Ulysses*."

Farzin said, "Our story is very similar to one of Saadi's."

Azad said, "How was that?"

Farzin said, "There's a story in the Golestan book that is about an astronomer: one day he comes home and finds out that his wife is sitting with another man. He starts to scream and hit her. Then people gather at his door to find out what has happened. A wise man is passing by. Someone tells him the story. The man says, 'If this man doesn't know what's going on in his own household, how is he to find out about the stars in the universe?' And so our story is similar to that of the astronomer."

A FALL AFTERNOON IN THE PARK

*A*REZOO AND ARMAN ARE SITTING on a bench in the park. Their twins, Shadi and Omid, are swinging a few metres away. It's the middle of the fall and a cold wind is blowing. There're no other children in the playground.

Arezoo spreads a napkin on the bench, between Arman and herself, takes out of a bag half a cake that was made the same day. She also takes out the tea flask along with four plastic cups and puts them on the bench. She divides the cake into three portions and gives the bigger one to Arman, leaving the other two for the children.

Arman takes a bite of the cake and brings the cup of tea to his mouth to drink. He looks at Arezoo, who puts a cube of sugar in her mouth and drinks some tea.

"What about you? Don't you want to have cake?"

"No, I already had some. In the morning when I baked it, I ate a big piece."

Arman says nothing and eats his cake in silence.

The sky is covered with grey clouds, but there's no sign of rain, only the smell of smog. The fallen leaves on the ground move with the wind this way and that way, like drifters who don't know where they are off to.

A beggar is walking toward them. When he reaches them, he stops for a while. There is the same vagrancy in his eyes that is in his condition. Arezoo opens her purse to give him some money. The man doesn't stop and continues on his way. A crow's croak breaks the park's silence. A black cat with a white spot on its head appears from behind a tree and disappears slowly. A little farther on, a young girl and boy are sitting on a bench, their heads close to each other.

To break the silence, Arezoo says, "Look at them. It seems the world is in their favour."

"Why not? When you're young, the world is in your favour."

"Like us, when the world was in our favour."

Arman says nothing. He looks at the young boy and girl. It seems the boy is reading something from a book that is open on his knees.

The silence sits between them like an unwanted guest. They look at the children. It feels as if there are unsaid words between them, words that are hard to say. A cold wind blows and the tree branches stir with a rustle. Arezoo wraps the scarf that had covered her hair around her shoulders.

Arman takes his eyes from the children who are both just standing still, as if they are tired of playing. He looks at Arezoo and says, "If you feel cold, we can go."

"No, I don't feel cold. We just arrived, why should we go? Let the children be together for a while. They haven't had their tea and cake yet."

Arman says nothing and again there's silence between them.

Arezoo looks at the children, who seem to be talking together, but their voices don't reach Arezoo and Arman.

Arman finishes his cake and drinks from his tea. He looks at Arezoo and asks, "What's new?"

With the cup of tea in her hand, Arezoo says, "Nothing."

And after a while she asks, "What about you?"

And she reads the same answer in his eyes: *Nothing*.

A heavy silence like a dark cloud sits between them again. A woman covered by a black chador, with only her eyes and nose visible, crosses in front of them. The noise of her heavy steps breaks the quiet.

Arezoo drinks her tea, releases a deep breath from her chest and says, "Do you know Mr. Seraji?"

Arman, as if hasn't heard Arezoo's words, says, "I never have been in the park this time of year," then looks at Arezoo and asks, "Don't you feel cold?"

And after a while, as if he just then heard what Arezoo said, he asks, "What did you say?"

She says, "I said, 'Do you know Mr. Seraji?' The one who went to Canada on a mission and didn't come back? The story was in the newspapers as well. He was your classmate in the university, wasn't he?"

"Yes, he was. What do you mean?"

"His sister, Ms. Talaat, is looking for someone to go to their house and take care of her mother. It seems her mother had a stroke and she's paralyzed. Yesterday she called and talked to Maman and said they are looking for someone. She said, if Arezoo agrees to do it, they won't look for someone else. She said …"

"Well, it's enough. Don't continue. Does she really ask that you go to her mother's place and take care of her? Why she doesn't take care of her mother herself?"

"She has a husband and small children. I think her house is very far from her mother's house, maybe in a suburb of Tehran. She also works; I believe she is an engineer. Her husband has an export and import company."

"She gave your mother so much information to hire you to take care of her mother? She might want to compensate for her brother's conscience. The asshole was working like a spy. This woman's brother, who you think was my friend—yes, that Ahmad Seraji—reported against me and that was the reason I was expelled from the university, and then …"

"Then you didn't want to continue. Or it might be because of me sticking to you."

"No, it wasn't your fault. To tell the truth, because I was away from university for so long, I wasn't in the mood to continue my education. Imagine if I had become an engineer—nothing would be changed. You get nowhere with this kind of job in this country."

There was silence between them again. After a while, Arman looks at Arezoo, who was looking at the children, and he says,

A FALL AFTERNOON IN THE PARK

"Then, so. Ahmad Seraji's sister wants to hire you to be a maid …"

Arezoo interrupts Arman abruptly, saying, "What do you mean, 'be a maid'? Maman was saying that she'd heard that I'd lost my job. She wanted to help."

Silence clouded over them again.

Arman looks at Arezoo after a while and with an angry face asks her, "Did you accept it?"

Arezoo says nothing.

Arman raises his voice and says, "Aren't they really ashamed of themselves, proposing you take a job an illiterate person can do? Don't you have a nursing certificate? It seems that they have forgotten about who their father was, and now claim that they are the offspring of a king. I remember their house, in a poor neighbourhood—just about fifty square metres and with six or seven children."

"Yes, now those six or seven children all have become somebody. All of them have studied in university…"

"Perhaps after the revolution, when the door of the university opened to these kinds of people and all of them were accepted with a bribe and a letter from the government officials. And now all of them have become somebody. Why haven't I gotten anywhere?"

"And you, please don't remember the past. Just tell me what you think. They said they will pay me what I ask."

Arman raises his voice but tries not to be insulting, and says, "Ms. Educated Nurse. How do you permit yourself to accept such a job? Haven't you been a supervisor of a ward in a public hospital? Are you ready now to work at the level of an illiterate person? Imagine, she's the mother of such and such person, who has been somebody after the revolution and their wealth …"

Anger stops Arman from continuing. He looks far away, to the street, where cars have filled up the spots; the smell of their smog reaches the park. After a while he continues: "Perhaps your maman has told them that you've lost your job and now you and Shadi are a burden on them. And then she wants to have a favour and proposes this job to you. You would probably have to change her diaper and wash her ass as well."

Arezoo doesn't answer. She drinks her tea. The girl and boy who were sitting on the bench have left. She looks at the children; it seems they are talking together again.

She says hesitantly, "I haven't accepted yet."

Arman says nothing.

After a while, with suffocated anger in his voice, Arman asks, "What happened to your complaint?"

"Nothing yet. The private hospital has asked for a letter from my previous workplace. None of them dare hire me. With those accusations—a failure to adhere to Islamic dress code, being rude ..."

And after a while she continues, "Unchaste. The bastard ..."

Arman raises his voice and says, "And you did a good job with what you told him."

"Of course I did. I humiliated him in front of patients and nurses, and cursed him with dirty words."

"You were lucky that they didn't arrest you for insulting the prophet."

"If they did, it wouldn't be much worse than this kind of life."

She turns her face away from Arman to not let him see her tears. She looks at a person crossing the narrow line between the trees.

Shadi puts her feet on the ground and stops her swing. Omid follows her and stops his as well. They stare at each other for a while as if they want to see the other better and keep them in their memories. A sadness prevents them from playing hide-and-seek and running around, something that they usually do when they come to the park. Their swinging doesn't last more than a few minutes, as if their minds are busy with something more important than playing.

Shadi looks at Omid for a while and then says hesitantly, "If Grandmother dies, Maman and I can come to Grandfather's place and live with you and Baba."

"What about Grandfather?"

"Grandfather can live with us too. Maman says someone has to take care of Grandfather and Maman will do that. Then all of us live together again, like the time we lived in that apartment."

"What about if Grandmamman dies earlier? Then Baba and I will come to Grandbaba's place and all of us will live together. Grandbaba also can't live by himself if Grandmaman dies. Someone has to make lunch and dinner for him."

"Well, Maman is here. And I don't think that Grandbaba accepts my baba. I heard him telling Maman that her husband is a careless man. He shouldn't have left that apartment without getting some money from its owner."

"But don't believe that Grandmother and Grandfather are very kind to us. I heard Grandfather saying to Baba that what happened to us was because of Maman. He said she spent money lavishly, and went to work with heavy makeup on until they expelled her from the hospital. She didn't let you buy a forty-square-metre apartment for yourself. You lived so long in a rental apartment until you were thrown out on the street and became a vagabond. I asked Grandbaba, what is a vagabond? He screamed at me, 'Leave me alone, kid. You've become like a burden on my neck.' To tell the truth, I can't understand half of his words. Do you remember a while ago, when they were kind to us? Whenever we went to visit, they had chelo kabab, bought from a restaurant. But now there is no chelo kabab anymore, just boiled chicken or a dish without meat. If I complain, Grandmother says, 'We have blood pressure, kid.' But, well, tell me the truth, do you prefer if Grandmother dies first or Grandmaman?"

"Honestly, I'd like Grandmother to die first. Not that I really want her to die. I love her a lot. But, well, since we've lived in Grandmaman's place, we don't have a good time. I mean, they aren't kind to us anymore. Grandbaba was saying to Maman that they weren't clever enough to buy a twenty-square-metre apartment for themselves. Grandmaman also won't let my maman watch her TV shows at night. We sleep in the living room and Maman can't stay awake late at night. She has to turn the light off and doesn't have the right to watch TV in those hours. Sometimes I realize that Maman is crying. I really don't know why Grandmaman and Grandbaba changed. Do you remember those times when we lived in our apartment? Whenever they invited us for lunch or dinner how much love they gave us? Now Grandbaba just praises Mr. Nasser. He says he was a clever man to take his family to America. He says, Mr. Naser was an intelligent man. I didn't understand what 'intelligent' meant. Do you know what 'intelligent' means?"

"No, I don't know either. It might be foreign currency. Yes, Mr. Nasser was rich. Do you remember whenever he came to our birthday party, what a big gift he brought for us?"

"Happy Nasim and Bashar. Maman showed me their pictures on Facebook—without hijab and in colourful dresses."

"They might live in a big apartment and have separate bedrooms, as well."

"Not like us; two in our grandfather's and two in our grandbaba's.

"And they aren't waiting for their grandfather to die until they can live all together again."

Note

The meaning of the characters' names in Farsi:
Arezoo: Wish
Arman: Ideal
Shadi: Joy
Omid: Hope

RAINY DAY

I REMEMBER FROM THE TIME I was a little girl the day my father would bring home his monthly pay. That day was special for us. He sometimes brought us a small box of pastry, just one for each, not more. He gave some of his wages to my mother for daily expenses and set aside part for a rainy day. I always imagined my father a generous man.

When I was a child, I didn't have a clear image of a rainy day, but I imagined it as unique. I sometimes dreamt about that day, the day I could get what I wished to have. If I asked for a new pair of shoes or a new dress or even a new notebook with the red cover, I was told, no, it's not possible. The money is not for buying a new pair of shoes or a new dress or even an extra notebook if you don't need them. We have to save it for a rainy day. With my childish imagination I dreamt that with the money that my father saved for the rainy day, we'd be rich one day, and every year I could have a new school uniform, shiny new shoes, a new overcoat and new winter boots like many of my classmates.

In those days when I dreamed about the rainy day, my brother was very young and didn't have any conception of poverty. He didn't go to school and his demands were merely to have food or the cheap toys my mother bought him from the street vendors, which made him happy. But for me, since I was eight or nine years old, I had big dreams in my head.

Before, when I was four or five or maybe younger, when my brother still couldn't walk and I was three years older than him, or, precisely, three years and eight months older, I wished to have a doll. I had seen it in the window of one of the city shops—sitting in a row with golden, brown or black hair and dresses in different colours and different styles. Whenever we passed the main square where the big shops were located and I asked for that doll, my mother or father again told me the same thing: that the money they were saving for a rainy day wasn't for buying a doll. The doll I liked had golden hair. Having golden hair, even in my childhood, was a special beauty. It might have been because my aunt, my father's sister, and her daughters had golden hair and my mother and her sisters dyed their hair gold. Even though I hadn't any understanding of gold, I could imagine it was a precious thing.

I remember once when I insisted too much that my mother and father buy me one of those dolls. My mother didn't pay too much attention to my begging. As folks say, she heard it with one ear and let it go out the other. But my father made me sit on his knee and pretended that he was interested in what I was asking for. I talked about the doll in detail and mentioned her golden hair. He listened to me—or not—and after a while he sent me away. When my mother told me to be a nice girl, I begged her, "If I'm a good girl, will you buy me that doll?"

So year after year passed and that doll stayed in the window of that shop, or perhaps it was sold and a new one replaced it.

I remember that after I started school sometimes I talked with my classmates about the dolls we had. When I heard that some of them had that kind of doll, my desire for having one made me dream about owning one. But after a while I stopped asking my parents to buy one for me. I knew that it was useless. The doll became inaccessible for me and I could have it only in my dream.

I was in grade two when I got sick and one day when I had a high fever, my mother promised me when I got well she'd buy me one of those dolls. I got well but still there was no doll for me. One day when I pleaded, my mother said, "Honey, your father doesn't earn enough money to buy expensive toys for you. If some money is left from our home expenses, he saves it for a rainy day."

And I still had the same idea about the rainy day that I had when I was three or four years old, imagining that day was reachable. I asked my mother, "Is it possible to go to the rainy day?" She asked, "Go where?"

I said, "Let's go to the rainy day. Father has saved lots of money for that day. He can buy me a doll with that money."

My mother laughed loudly and then said, "My dear daughter, the rainy day isn't a special place. God forbid that we reach the rainy day. The rainy day isn't a day when we have lots of money. The rainy day is a day when your father loses his job or gets sick or, God forbid, he dies ... Never wish for us to get to the rainy day."

What my mother said scared me and after that I tried not to think about the rainy day. As I became older, the doll was no longer in my dreams, but my father still brought home his monthly wage and gave part of it to my mother for our daily expenses and saved part of it for the rainy day, as he said.

When I was in the last year of high school, being a doctor was my utmost dream. I was sure that if I passed the entrance exam for medical school, my parents would be so happy, and with the money that my father had saved for the rainy day, he would be able to pay the cost of me studying in Tehran.

I hadn't yet finished my final high school exams when my father had a stroke and passed away within a week.

His burial and memorial were like a nightmare. I passed the final exams for high school, with a very good mark, which surprised even myself. I registered for the universities' entrance exam and thought about the rainy day. Actually, the rainy day was very close. I told my mother, "If I'm accepted at the university, you can pay for my expenses with the money that Father saved."

In the two months after my father's death, my mother aged suddenly. She didn't cry but she was mostly angry and depressed. And she directed her anger at my brother and me, as if we had brought on the death of our father.

One Friday, at the beginning of summer, after we had our breakfast, my mother talked to my brother and me. Bitterly she said, "I have to talk to you. You should know everything." My mother looked at my brother and me and said, "Your father's death was a catastrophe." And then she was quiet for a while, as if she couldn't continue.

"Catastrophe" to me meant something terrible. I don't know how my brother reacted to this news. Being younger than me, he might not have had such a dire feeling, but for me it was as if a dark curtain covered my eyes.

Mother said, "Your father didn't leave a penny for us ..."

I interrupted my mother and asked, "What about the money he saved for the rainy day?"

With the same bitterness, she said, "Nothing."

Her saying "nothing" was such a disappointment that my brother and I became paralyzed and didn't know what to say. I pulled myself from that abyss and said, "What about his pension?"

My mother said, "He had no pension."

My father had changed his job once in a while and each time he explained that his wage wasn't enough or his boss didn't treat him properly. Finally he was happy with his last job, and his salary. He said there was a good chance of promotion for him. My father always got a new job before quitting his previous job.

That day, our family meeting finished with no resolution, but I talked to my mother in private and asked her, "What are you going to do?" Again I talked about father's pension. My mother said impatiently, "I told you, he had no pension. I suppose he cashed in all his pensions when he quit his job to start a new one."

I dared to ask, "Did Father have another wife or children?"

"I don't know. If he had, so far nobody has come forward."

And after a while she continued, "No, I don't think so. Your father always came home at night. Sometimes very late, but I don't remember that he ever spent a night away from home."

I said, "What about the money that he saved for a rainy day?"

Impatient, my mother said, "How do I know? Perhaps he spent it on self-indulgences. Your father was a prodigal man. When he was with his friends he was the one whose hand always went to his pocket and paid for the table. But I really don't know what happened to the money that he saved for the rainy day."

I asked, "What about me?" The university exams were a month away. I wanted to compete and I wanted to go to university, even if I had to borrow from my aunts or uncles.

My mother said nothing.

My uncle, my mother's brother who lived in Tehran, helped me. He bought me a round-trip ticket to Tehran and I was able to participate in the entrance exams. With the marks I obtained, I was able to choose any faculty in any university; I could study medicine at Tehran University. But there was no way that I could pay for the cost of living and studying in Tehran. My uncle insisted I stay with them, but he lived with his wife and two small children in a tiny apartment in the suburbs, far from the university. So I chose nursing in a college in the city where we lived and so I didn't have to leave home.

Sometimes I had a chat with my father in my dreams, saying that if he hadn't spent the savings for the rainy day now he could be proud of me, studying medicine at the University of Tehran, the most prestigious university in Iran. When I brought my report card home, he looked at it with pride and showed it to my mother and said, "Bahar should be a doctor, Dr. Bahar Radnia." And I looked with love at my father, who encouraged me to study hard and I dreamed about the day that I would be a doctor.

Anyway, a few months after my father's death my mother got a job in a restaurant and I got a part-time job in a doctor's office. Eventually, my brother finished high school and was accepted in engineering in one of the cities that wasn't too far from our city. My mother and I promised him we would pay his expenses.

In the last year of my studies, I was on duty in the hospital one night when a paralyzed man who had had a stroke was brought in. His wife was with him and when she heard my family name, she looked at me with curiosity and asked me what was my relationship to Mr. Radnia.

I said, "He was my father."

"How many sisters and brothers have you?"

Her question surprised me. It wasn't her business how many brothers and sisters I had.

I asked her, "Did you know my father, I mean, Mr. Radnia?"

The nurse had taken her husband inside the ward and she was waiting in the hall. She breathed deeply and said, "Very well."

It didn't cross my mind that my father might have had a relationship with a paralyzed man's wife and spent the money he saved for the rainy day on her.

When the woman noticed the surprise in my face, she said, "My husband and your father were friends since they were in elementary school. And when they grew up, both of them were working in the same construction company. My husband fell from a tall scaffolding and became paralyzed. Since then it was your father who always helped us with our household expenses."

I asked her, "How many children do you have?"

"Just one daughter. She's a year younger than you—Jaleh Naseri. The one who has blond hair. You might not have seen her hair under her hijab."

"Yes, I've seen her hair, it's so beautiful."

And I remembered the doll with the blond hair.

Perhaps whenever I asked him to buy me that doll with blond hair, my father was thinking of the blond daughter of his friend who had fallen from a height and had been paralyzed. And my father spent his rainy day savings on his friend.

The anger and hatred that I had had for my father after his death were replaced by love and respect. The father who had pretended to be concerned about his own rainy day in reality was spending that money on his friend's family, whose needs were urgent.

Mr. Naseri was in the hospital for a week. One night when I was working the night shift, his situation became worse and he died before dawn.

My mother and I went to his memorial. When I talked about his life to my mother, she couldn't believe that her husband had cut back from his own family expenses to pay for his friend's necessities. But I believed Jaleh's mother had respected my father for taking responsibility for his friend.

A few months after Mr. Naseri's death, I was working on a patient's wound when I was paged. I answered the phone and I recognized Jaleh's mother's voice. I was surprised that she wanted to reach me so late at night. She said she'd like to see me.

"What for?"

"I can't talk by phone. But I would like to invite you to my place for a lunch or dinner, and then we'll talk."

I was waiting for her to invite my mother as well, but she didn't mention her.

At home when I talked about Jaleh's mother's invitation, my mother said, "Go and find out what her relationship with your father was. Even though ..."

And she didn't continue.

A week later I went to her home for lunch. She lived in a tiny two-room apartment. When I asked about her daughter, she said she was working in a clothing boutique.

I asked, "Won't she be home for lunch?"

"No."

She served me first with a cup of tea, then, sitting beside me, she said, "To tell the truth, I prefer to see you alone and talk to you. I'm going to talk about a secret that should stay between you and me. Promise me that you won't talk about it since I'm living, but after me it's up to you ..."

After I had my tea, she spread a tablecloth on the floor and served a dish of rice mixed with green beans and ground meat. During the lunch my mind was wandering and I hadn't a clue of what Jaleh's mother wanted to tell me. The only thought that didn't cross my mind was what Jaleh's mother, who introduced herself as Razieh, told me.

The silence stretched out, and whenever I looked at her, she looked away. I found myself saying, "Well ..."

She stopped eating, looked straight into my eyes and in a voice that was slightly trembling said, "I know you might not believe me, but it's true. Jaleh is your sister; the daughter of Satar Radnia."

She was right: I couldn't believe her. For a second I thought that she'd lost her wits and was living under an illusion. I thought she might have been under stress because of her husband's death. But then she continued in a faint voice, "You knew that my husband was paralyzed. It happened when we were newly married. He fell from a scaffolding. And when that accident happened to my husband, your father spent time with us. He had already married and your mother was pregnant with you. But he visited us almost every night to be with his friend and help him to recover. Then ..."

She stopped talking and looked out of the window.

"What about then ...?"

"Don't consider me one of those women ..."

I looked at her and said nothing.

She looked at me with compassion, like a mother looking at her own child, and said, "Jaleh is your sister. You don't have a sister, do you?"

Dumbfounded, I looked at her and couldn't believe what she was saying. The food was the worst I had ever eaten.

The silence stretched between us and then she said, "Yes, she's your sister. Jaleh has no other sister or brother, not even an uncle or aunt from my side. My other relatives aren't living in Iran. Since I got to know you, I'm telling myself, when I die ..."

For the first time I looked at her with curiosity, as if I wanted to know her better and have a clear image of her face. Then I noticed that she looked more fragile than the first day I had seen her. I thought it was because of her husband's death and perhaps my father's death, who had been like a breadwinner for them.

Unconsciously, I was staring at her and thinking about the rainy day and all my dreams that had faded. I thought about that doll with blond hair and then Jaleh's hair, which wasn't similar to her mother's hair nor my father's, but to my aunt's—my father's sister, golden as gold. And my father had not only spent his savings for our rainy day, but had also given the colour of his sister's hair to his other daughter.

There was a burning anger inside me, though I didn't know toward whom I was angry. Toward my father, who stole all my childish dreams, depriving me of a small doll, or a notebook? Or toward this woman, who stole part of my father's wages, which should have been spent on his wife and his children, and on my education?

As if she read my thoughts, she said, "I didn't want talk about it and hurt you, but …"

With hatred, I asked, "But what?"

"I'm sick, too. I have liver cancer and may die in a year or even less."

I looked at her but still I hated her. I couldn't swallow my food. I hadn't eaten more than a few spoonfuls.

Mrs. Razieh looked at my plate and said, "I shouldn't have talked about this before lunch."

AN APARTMENT FOR SAHAND

I'D KNOWN HAJAGHA MOJTABA since we were kids. Then his name was Mehran, Mehran Mavadat. Mehran is a name that can be given to both girls and boys. Mehran had wavy, light-brown hair and pale skin. He had twin sisters called Mitra and Mandana, who had blond hair. His mother, my mother believed, coloured her hair blond; she also always wore heavy makeup. We lived in the same alley and went to the same school, but after the revolution they sold their house and left our neighbourhood.

His father was an army colonel, and as my father said, he must have been fired from the army after the revolution and they probably immigrated to another country, as many did. I didn't have any news from Mehran until a few months ago, when my father passed away, and I saw him in the neighbourhood mosque for my father's memorial. After the ceremony we stopped to exchange a few words. He introduced himself and said he knew me from the past. He consoled me for my father's death. He was very friendly, saying he used to live in this neighbourhood with his parents and we had been classmates. He said he had quit school when he was in grade eleven, and was on the front line for a while. He had wanted to join the Revolutionary Guards but his father was against it. So now he was running a few mosques' affairs. He said he was married and had four children. When I said I had only one son, he looked at me with a kind of surprise and said nothing, but when I told him I was living in my father's house, which had been converted to an apartment building with four units, one of which I own, he looked at me with sympathy and asked me what I was doing.

I said, "I'm a high school teacher and sometimes I write articles for one of the weekly journals and sometimes short stories."

"You can't live on these kinds of jobs."

"My wife is working, too," I said with pride.

He laughed loudly and continued, "Women's salaries are so low that they are barely enough for their personal expenses such as dresses and some necessities."

I said to myself, *What kind of dress?* Anyway, teachers have to wear a special dress which is not really a dress.

When he was saying goodbye, he asked to see me again, since once we had been neighbours, classmates and friends.

Even though he was kind and trying to be friendly, I didn't want to socialize with him. I didn't remember having been friends with him; I remembered my parents saying his parents were arrogant and stayed away from other neighbours. And now Hajagha Mojtaba seemed to be someone important in our neighbourhood.

When I told the story to Mojgan, she said, "He must be a loyal friend who has not forgotten you after so many years and still appreciates the old friendship."

Surprised, I said, "What kind of friendship?"

I told her about his parents and their house, which was at the end of the alley and was bigger than all the other houses in the quarter. It has been changed into a twelve-storey building now. But in those days, there were houses in the alley and the walls were covered with jasmine honeysuckle. The neighbourhood was filled with its perfume during the spring and summer. They had a big yard with the large building at the end. I told her about his twin sisters, who wore miniskirts before the revolution and always looked elegant. Their blond hair reached their shoulders and they were very attractive. We teenage boys used to watch them wistfully. Then when the revolution happened, they were the first ones to wear hijab. The colonel's wife even had a chador, but she still had the same arrogant and haughty behaviour. With Mehran it was different. He was friendly and popular at school and always spent money on his friends, although I wasn't one of them because there was a big gap between our social classes.

My wife asked me now, "Are you talking about Hajagha Mojtaba, the fixer in the mosque?"

"His name then was Mehran. And because he had brown hair and brown eyes and a pale complexion, sometimes kids at school called him Ms. Mehran. How do you know him?"

"Is it possible to live in this neighbourhood and not know Hajagha Mojtaba? You have to deal with him if you go to the mosque to ask for something."

A week later, when I got home one day, Mojgan said Hajagha Mojtaba had called and wanted to talk to me. I wondered why he had called and what he wanted from me.

Anyway, I phoned him the next day. He talked to me for a while about the time when we were in the same school, and then, a little cautiously, said he would like to see me.

I said he could come to my place if he liked, though my tone wasn't friendly.

He laughed loudly and said, "Don't be so formal with me. We have been classmates, neighbours and friends and have eaten each other's bread and butter."

I asked myself, *Bread and butter?* I didn't remember going to his house, or him coming to ours. In those times Mehran was a colonel's son and lived in a big house, and my father was a vice principal in an elementary school; our house was much smaller compared to theirs. And now he was talking about bread and butter. Maybe he was referring to the halva and dates that were served at my father's memorial?

He asked if I was free on Friday night after evening prayer, for a short visit. "Please don't put your wife in trouble. I just want to have a cup of tea with you and talk about the past and confabulate."

I answered, "My wife won't be home on Friday night. She is going to a gathering with her friends."

"Good."

I felt a little anxious. Even all these years after the revolution, I did my best to stay away from people connected with the government as well as new Muslims, Revolutionary Guards, and clergy. As folks say, I tried to live on my hard work and not be in debt to anyone.

My son, Sahand, had finished his education and was engaged to a college mate who was still a student. They were waiting to buy a small apartment to start their life together. But given my income and his mother's and what he made, buying an apartment, even in a very cheap neighbourhood, was only a dream. But as Mojgan used to say, God is great. There was no need to be friends with people like Mehran Mavadat, or as Mojgan called him, Hajagha Mojtaba. When his father was someone in our neighbourhood, he didn't consider me his friend and I didn't know why he wanted to befriend me now.

When I talked to Mojgan about my concerns, she said, "Since you don't know what his intention is, you'd better see him. Meeting your friend, or as you call him your old neighbour and classmate, won't hurt you. Plus, I don't think he wants to propose you for a position in their organization. These kinds of people don't trust their own father and you are a stranger to them."

I asked her, "You've seen him a few times. What kind of person do you think he is?"

She looked at me, surprised, and said, "What a question. What I know is that he's a fixer in the mosque. But he's not a bad person, nor is he foul-mouthed. He's not like many others, who consider the whole country as their father's property. He helps people as much as he can and doesn't make it harder for them. He doesn't send them back empty-handed."

"With what you said, it seems okay to let him come here. I just hope he won't ask me for anything."

Mojgan laughed bitterly and said, "Do you have something that he would ask for? These kinds of people have more than enough. The donations they collect for the charity fund, it's a great wealth. Whenever I want to put money in the charity boxes, they are so full that I have to push hard to put my money in."

"Then why do you do it?"

With the same bitterness, she continued, "I don't know. I always donate to these charity boxes and hope the money reaches someone in need."

To encourage her not to be disappointed, I said, "I hope so, too."

That night, Mojgan brewed some tea and arranged the table with a dish of pastry and some fruits, then left. Sahand had a few students he was teaching mathematics to and would not return home until late at night. So, the whole apartment was mine—waiting for my old classmate Mehran Mavadat, or Hajagha Mojtaba, as he was called.

He showed up half an hour late. He had stubble that was more white than black and his suit didn't look very new. He behaved with warmth and intimacy, as if we had been close friends for years.

He sat down and I offered him tea, sweets and fruit. But the first thing I noticed was a big bag that he kept beside himself when he settled on the couch; once in a while he caressed it as if there was something live and dear in it that needed attention. I could not guess what could be in it.

Hajagha Mojtaba was cordial and talkative. He didn't stop talking for a second—talking about this and that. He didn't mention politics, the high cost of living or the government or the mosques' affairs or anything related to these two organizations. He talked about his own family, about his twin sisters, who were in the U.S. He said, "Both of them married, almost at the same time, two brothers who were studying in America but were here for a short visit with their parents. It was God's will that they married brothers. My father knew their family from the past and they were reliable people. They left the country for their destinies. Both of them studied at the university and got a degree. But I don't know exactly what they are doing now."

He continued, "As my parents say, it seems they have a good life. I have not been to the U.S. yet but my parents travelled there several times. They were able to get their green cards and stayed there. My parents believe that life in America is abundance ... They asked me to go there. Especially my mother, who calls me and says she's missing her granddaughters. But she has grandchildren over there, too. She almost raised my two older daughters. My wife was sick mostly and my mother was lonely and missed her daughters very much, so she helped my wife with our kids."

Hajagha Mojtaba talked non-stop, all about his life, and I was getting bored. I asked myself, why do I have to listen to this? And I was wondering, what does he want from me?

Then he talked about his second marriage. He said, "My wife got sick after her second delivery but she gave birth to a third child. She wanted to have a son. Yes, I wanted to have a son, too. Without a son, it seems that there's something missing in your life. You know that having a son is something else. You have a son and you know that if you have ten daughters, you still need to have a son. Our third child was a boy. He wasn't even two years old when my wife got pregnant again. The doctor had warned her that she shouldn't get pregnant. But she did and she wanted to have another son. As if getting pregnant with a boy or girl was in her own control. That one was a girl and my wife got more sick. The doctor warned her again that getting pregnant could mean death for her. She was still determined to give birth again. What should I do then? So, I had to have another wife. Not that I divorced my first wife. She'd changed to a nagging and sick person always in a bad mood. She didn't treat our children nicely. I wanted to divorce her but I thought I would lose my reputation. My father-in-law is somebody in the government and I had to consider that. I am somebody, too, I mean financially I am in a good shape. Look at this bag. It's full of money—cash. The money of charity boxes. I'm trusted by people."

I looked at the bag, which was lying beside Hajagah Mojtaba's leg like an obedient, mute and deaf creature. I could hear the prayers of my wife and other women as they pushed large and small notes into the charity box, hoping that their wishes might come true. So this was the same money. But what was this money doing in my home?

Maybe Hajagha Mojtaba carried the money with him wherever he went, or perhaps he couldn't leave it at home—he might not trust his wives.

I was busy with my thoughts when Hajagha Mojtaba interrupted me. It was as if he was talking to himself and didn't care whether I was listening. He said, "Do you know, brother …"

For the first time he called me "brother." No one called you sir anymore. You mostly were a brother rather than a sir.

Yes, Hajagha Mojtaba was saying that his wife complained too much and after her fourth delivery was sick and though the doctors prohibited her from having more children, she still wanted to have another son. "So, I thought about having another wife. I didn't say anything to my wife. I didn't have the patience for a quarrel. I told you, my father-in-law is somebody and he is a hard-liner. I'm afraid of him. He is important and after the revolution he's stronger and he runs one of the city upper area's mosques. Well, I had to stand by my wife. But when God and the prophet say that a Muslim man can have four wives and I had a religious reason—my wife couldn't perform her marital duties. So, I got married again, without shame. Well, she is much younger than my other wife, almost the same age as my older daughter. But she's happy; me, too. And now she's pregnant—with a boy."

And this time he laughed contentedly.

Hajagha Mojtaba's behaviour changed slowly. The talkative, good man became a thousand-faced man, an opportunist and even a cruel man. As if he could read my thoughts on my face, he looked at his watch and said, "I've talked too much. But the main reason for my visit …"

He stroked the bag with his hand, looked around our sixty-square-metre apartment and said, "In fact, the reason for troubling you is that I have to go on a trip for a few days and I wanted to leave this bag with you." He looked into my eyes to see my reaction.

As I watched him with surprise, he said, "This is the money from the charity boxes. This is people's money and they have trusted me with it and I want to leave it with you for a few days. There's an emergency trip. I can't leave the money with my wives. I mean, either of them. You know how women are. They are not trustworthy. No matter what you do, they are not honest with you. Malignancy is in their natures."

His words were maddening because he was insulting my wife and all women. Even though I knew he was talking about his own wives, I was about to interrupt him, when he patted his stubble and looked straight into my eyes and continued, "Yes, just for a few days. But I want to ask you not to say a word to your wife. Women can't keep a secret. If they don't tell it to a person, then they will talk about it to a well. As folks say, a wall has a mouse and a mouse has ears. If you tell your wife, she will tell your son, or a friend or neighbour or one of the school's teachers who is like sister to her! Well, then it is only Khajeh Hafez Shiraz who doesn't know the secret, and he usually finds out through his ghezels, when one wants to ask him for an omen." He laughed loudly.

I was wondering whether I should laugh or not. I was getting bored with his talk, his jumping from one subject to another. I could imagine people who go to mosque learn from their mullahs to talk a lot and mostly nonsense. It was close to Mojgan's time to return home. I looked at my watch and he got the idea. I sensed that all the stories he had told me were to gain my trust and to show his good humour.

At first I thought I should say no. I didn't have anything to do with the mosque. But as Mojgan said, Hajagha Mojtaba was "someone" in the mosque, and for sure he had connections with people who were in top positions in the government. It was possible that I would be in trouble if I refused. His request, I told myself, keeping a bag of money for a few days, wouldn't be a problem. But this was the only thing I'd do for him and I'd have to tell him that I was not looking for trouble. But I didn't say it, and instead I said, "Your money will be safe with me. And I will not share this secret with my wife or son."

With a smile he said, "Don't be so formal with me. We're buddies."

I just smiled back.

It was close to eleven when he left and the bag remained with me. He didn't even open it to show me the money. I didn't ask him to, either. When he left, I put the bag in a closet and when Mojgan returned home, the first thing I told her was about the bag full of money that was in the corner of our closet. I brought the bag out and opened it. There wasn't any lock on it. When Mojgan saw the stacks of large and small bills, with fear in her eyes, she said, "I'm scared to look at them, as if they were poisonous snakes squirming into each other. Take it away from my eyes. Leave it in a place that I don't have to see it. Be careful that Sahand won't notice it or he might have a temptation to open it."

I said, "I'd better leave it under my bed. That is a safer place."

"Yes, you'd better hide it somewhere else, where I won't be able to see it."

Three days later, Mojgan, coming back from shopping, said, "Something terrible happened."

Worried, I asked, "What happened?"

Leaving her shopping bags on the kitchen counter, without taking her manteau off, she dropped her scarf on her shoulder, sat on a chair and continued, "In the grocery store someone said Hajagha Mojtaba was killed in an accident in Karaj-Tehran road." And then she asked me, "What are we going to do now?"

And the words jumped out of my mouth: "What do you mean, what do we do now? Were we the reason for his accident? There's nothing we can do."

"What about the bag full of money?"

Smiling, I said, "That is a gift from God. We can buy an apartment for Sahand and put his hand in Hanieh's, who has been waiting for five years."

Mojgan said nothing and started to put her groceries away.

When there was no one at home, I counted the money, and I realized I could afford a down payment for a small apartment in our neighbourhood. I would tell Sahand that I'd saved the money over the past few years.

Without telling Mojgan, I went to a real estate office and looked for an apartment that would be suitable. It took about two months before I found one that wasn't too far from our place. I talked to Mojgan about it, expecting her to be happy, but she looked at me as if she was looking at a fool, then asked me, "Do you really want to buy an apartment for Sahand?"

"Yes, with Hajagha Mojtaba's money."

Surprised, she asked, "Which money?"

"The money—"

She didn't let me finish my sentence. She brought out the bag, which wasn't puffy and heavy anymore. I took it from her hand and opened it. There were only two packs of bills inside.

Before I could ask her what she had done with the money, before I got angry and my voice turned harsh, she said, "I returned it to the charity box."

I asked, in a faint voice, "How?"

"One pack or two at a time, and dropped them in the box, where the money belongs."

Helpless, I looked at her and said nothing.

She left her hand on my shoulder and said, "I didn't like the last part of your story."

I DIDN'T KNOW HER

WHEN THE GUESTS WERE ALL GONE, Sepideh invited Nasim to sit down instead of starting to clean up. Nasim sat beside Sepideh on the sofa and looked around the room at the serving plates and crumpled-up paper napkins on top of small tables and the large dining table, where there rested empty and half-filled glasses, serving dishes and the salad bowl; chairs were left here and there.

Her furniture for the sitting room, and the dining table with its twelve high-back chairs, her heavy floral curtains layered with lace curtains, which made them seem cozier: these were signs of Sepideh's prosperous life. Sepideh had turned off the chandelier in the dining room, but there was light from table lamps that gave the living room a welcoming feel and made the mess less visible.

Nasim said, "You went to lots of trouble arranging this party. You should have let them tidy up before leaving."

Sepideh made herself comfortable beside Nasim and said, "I'll leave the cleaning for the morning. I won't touch anything now. I want to be with you in these few hours left of your visit. Tomorrow Shahnaz is coming back and will do the cleaning. Tonight she had to go home. Her husband won't let her stay overnight. Actually, I mostly wanted just us to be together these last hours, but when you said you would like to see your old friends, I'm sure I would have regretted it if I hadn't invited them. I wished you'd mentioned it earlier so I could have done it sooner, not on the last night of your trip. And now that you're leaving, God knows when you might come back."

Nasim took her eyes from Sepideh and looked at the painting hanging on the opposite wall, which was of a young girl in a colourful dress and a white hat who had curious eyes, as if she were listening to them.

Nasim looked at Sepideh again and said, "If I come back, it's not easy when I go back there. As if ..." She didn't continue. But she said to herself, "As if to be torn off, half here and half there."

Sepideh looked at Nasim, who seemed sad and exhausted. Her smile didn't mean anything.

Sepideh said, "Anyway, I think it was good that you came back. You know many of your friends had another perception of you. They thought you'd left behind your homeland and the people here. You know what I mean? They might imagine that because you've got some prestige and fame over there and achieved some success, you've forgotten about your roots and your past. They thought you've forgotten them."

Surprised, Nasim shook her head and said, "What words! Nonsense. It's not true at all. Everything I have is because of my past and the people I knew then. Is it possible to break with the past? Well, for a while I couldn't come back. I couldn't find a reason to travel here. But the past was going to disappear from my memory, my memories were fading. I wanted to see my childhood and teenage friends. I wanted to know about their lives, happy or not. You know what I mean by happiness—not just materialistic. Yes, you wrote me about some of them, but I needed to see them and talk to them and know more about their lives. It was important to me to hear their voices and have them talk to me about themselves.

Sepideh stared at Nasim for a while, as if she had something to say that she couldn't verbalize. The question had been with her since the day Nasim came back. She wasn't the same person who had left Iran. Sometimes she seemed like a stranger. Sometimes she sank into a deep silence and didn't pay attention to her or answer her questions. But if Sepideh asked about her life, Nasim would smile and say she was okay. Sepideh didn't know what that meant.

Nasim was mostly quiet and preoccupied rather than happy. Sepideh might even have said she was depressed.

Now that it was just two hours until her departure, the question was on Sepiedeh's tongue like a thorn and she thought she should ask Nasim about it. But it seemed she didn't have the courage. When the silence stretched between them, Sepideh finally asked, "Nasim, be honest with me. Are you really happy?" And she was surprised by her outspokenness. Since Nasim had returned, Sepideh hadn't found a chance to ask her about her life. She knew she was very sensible and it was perhaps because of her that she took refuge in creative work. Nasim was lucky that she had been able to achieve success in her field and she had a good life. And perhaps because of her fame many people came to see her. But when Sepideh scrutinized Nasim, she didn't find her happy, or proud of herself and her success, as if all the praise and admiration were for someone else. She only answered her admirers with a smile and sometimes said that they were boasting about her.

Nasim said, "Why are you asking me this question? I don't have a definition for happiness. How do you say someone is happy?"

"So you aren't happy?"

"I don't know. I told you, I don't know what happiness is and what it means. I just want to say, the thing that you call happiness cost me a lot. I have bargained all my life for it. I've never talked about what happened to me in exile. But, well, I don't have regrets. I think life is never easy when you have to uproot yourself unwillingly from your homeland. For me it has been hard and I've never thought about happiness."

After a while she said, "What do you think? Are you happy? Or your friends, which one of them is happy?"

Nasim's answer made Sepideh regret posing such a question to her. She hadn't expected Nasim's answer. People usually say in one sentence that they are happy, or not. Nasim, too, could have done the same. And then why, from the first day of her arrival, had she said that she'd achieved what she was looking for? But why wasn't she happy? It might be because of her past. She suddenly remembered Behrooz. During the three weeks that Nasim was with her, she hadn't mentioned him even once, as if he had never existed. But Nasim had been in love with Behrooz before leaving Iran, in the years when many of the young people had to live a hidden life. When Nasim left Iran, for a while she didn't have any news from Behrooz—he'd been captured and imprisoned by the government. Later, Sepideh read in the newspaper that he had been executed and she wrote the news to Nasim and couldn't understand how Nasim dealt with her sorrow in exile. She knew that Nasim had gone to Khavaran, where Behrooz was buried in a mass grave, without saying anything about it to Sepideh.

To change the subject, she said, "I hope all the people you wanted to meet were here. Ms. Akhtar's daughter also was here. I saw that you were talking to Ms. Akhtar's daughter. You'd told me that you would like to see her."

Nasim took her eyes from the painting of the young girl who was watching them and looked at Sepideh with surprise and said, "Which one was Ms. Akhtar? No one introduced her to me."

"There was no Ms. Akhtar. She passed away two years ago. But her daughter was here. I introduced her to you: Mrs. Rastegar. Don't you remember?"

"Mrs. Rastegar? You should have told me her first name."

"I thought you would recognize her. Her first name was Setareh. I saw you were talking to her. What were you talking about?"

"What about? About everything; mostly about exile. She wanted to know if exile is really exile. Yes, we talked but there was no hint of the past, that she knew me from the past. She didn't mention that I stayed with them for a while. She didn't say that when I wanted to leave the country, I had taken refuge in their house until things were ready for my departure. She didn't mention anything from the past. Mrs. Rastegar didn't bear any similarity to the girl I knew."

"Yes, she's aged, and that's natural."

"Yes, aging is natural, but why didn't I know her? What's her first name?"

"Setareh?"

"No, it's not Setareh. If I'm not mistaken, her name is Somayeh. We were in the same class. All the days and nights that I was in her house, she didn't leave me alone and asked me many questions. Some of her questions stayed with me for years. For example, do you know where you're going? Aren't you afraid to go by yourself? Sometimes she was like a boss to her mother and admonished her. I still remember how she looked at that time. But why I didn't know her? Nothing from that era was left in her."

And after a while, as if she was talking to herself, she said, "Somayeh? But why didn't I know her? Her mother had given me refuge."

"It might not be your fault."

"Whose was it then?"

"Well, you were tired, you were anxious. It was the last night of your visit. You should be at the airport soon. There are many of your friends that you might not remember very well. She also came late and left early. She didn't even stay for dinner."

"She left early because I didn't know her."

"Perhaps, but you ..."

"What about me?"

"You shouldn't feel bad about yourself. It wasn't your fault. She should have introduced herself to you. She should have talked about the past and the time you were at her parents' house."

"She didn't talk about the past, because she didn't want to mention that I'd taken refuge in their house. I had to remember and be thankful to her, her mother and father, who had given me refuge. She shouldn't have had to talk about it. I should have remembered."

Sepideh said nothing. And after a while, Nasim continued.

"Yes, human beings are forgetful. But why didn't I recognize her? She was my childhood friend. Yes, when we were children we were friends, but in high school we weren't friends any longer. She was the best in everything, in studying, in sports, and because of that I didn't like her. I was politically active and she wasn't. When I took refuge in their house I still didn't like her. But she was kind to me. She asked me lots of questions. She liked to talk to me, but I didn't consider her someone to talk to. Her mother was very kind to me also, but I ..."

"What about you?"

"Me, I don't know. I might have envied her. She had her own place and her mother who served her and I was homeless and had to leave my country and didn't know where I could take refuge. But in another way, I considered myself superior because I was involved in politics and the government was looking for me. I imagined I was more mature than she was. I mean, more experienced, while she was just busy with her school books, but later ..."

And after a while she continued, "Later on, when I was wiser, later on, I was ashamed of my behaviour. I told myself, whenever I see her again ... You know, I wasn't sure I'd see her again. And now I have come back and you made it possible for me to see her, so I could apologize to her and thank her for being so nice to me and for her mother's kindness and because of all those nights and days that I spent in their house they saved my life, and I ..."

"And what about you?"

Nasim looked Sepideh in the eye but it seemed she didn't see her. She continued, "I didn't recognize her."

At the airport, Sepideh stayed with Nasim until she checked her suitcases and got her boarding pass, and then they said goodbye.

Entering her apartment, it seemed to Sepideh that she had taken a heavy burden and delivered it safely to its destination. A few months earlier, when Nasim called to tell her she had gotten her passport and was going to travel to Iran, Sepideh was anxious that something might happen to her and for the three weeks that Sepideh was with her, the anxiety never left.

On her way home, she had thought she just wanted to go to bed and lie beside Parviz and have a nice sleep without any worries, but now at home, Sepideh could feel Nasim's absence and sadness covered her like a heavy cloud. But when she opened the door to the apartment, she found herself crossing the living room. The smell of the half-full dishes of rice and kabab and other foods filled the air. She pulled aside the curtains and opened the window. There were scattered clouds in the sky and the smell of rain in the twilight filled the apartment. Involuntarily she started to tidy up, putting the leftovers in containers. She became so busy with her work that her sadness paled. The twilight was alive behind the window. When she heard the sound of the doorbell, she thought she'd imagined it. But the second ring woke Parviz and brought him to the living room. Sepideh looked at him perplexed and said, "Who could it be?" And for a while it crossed her mind that they might have come to arrest Nasim, but she thanked God: "She has left."

When she checked the security camera, she saw the image of a woman she couldn't recognize at first glance in the street's weak light. When she heard Nasim's voice, she was scared to her bones. "For sure they have confiscated her passport and didn't let her board the plane." She pressed the button to open the door to the building and waited in the hallway for the elevator door to open.

It didn't take long for Nasim to emerge from the elevator, with her carry-on and her purse.

Bewildered, Sepideh didn't know what to say. With a smile, Nasim said, "I came back."

Standing by the apartment door, Sepideh couldn't find any words. Behind her Parviz said, "Why aren't you coming in?"

Sepideh gave way to let Nasim come in. She left her carry-on by the door, took her shoes off. Sepideh closed the door and asked, "What happened? They didn't let—"

Nasim didn't allow her to continue. She said, "I came back by myself."

"By yourself? Why?"

"I came back to apologize to Somayeh—oh no, Setareh, the daughter of Akhtar Khanum, who gave me refuge in that terrible time when I had no place to hide and no one dared give me shelter, when my life was in danger. I have to thank her."

"You came all the way back just for this?"

"Just for this."

SOMEONE WON, SOMEONE LOST

"Someone won, someone lost": an expression in Farsi

For my brother, Ali Akbar Yalfani,
who was like a father for me

I RECOGNIZED HIM AT FIRST GLANCE. I'm talking about Yousef, I mean Josef. He seemed to have changed his name here. He wasn't much different from the person I knew years ago in Iran; but more chubby, with a protruding belly that was partly hidden behind a huge, magnificent desk. He looked like a dwarf sitting on that shiny leather chair with its tall back. Yes, he had aged, but not as much as I would have expected.

I'd known him since my childhood. We were next-door neighbours back in Iran. His father had a grocery store in our neighbourhood and was also a big man with a potbelly. But his mother was a tall, slender, moody woman—we could hear her screaming at her children when she was in their yard. Whenever I saw her in the street, she was either pregnant or had a baby in her arms. There were eight children: two sisters and six brothers. One of the sisters was the eldest and the other one the youngest. The older sister, who was about thirteen or fourteen, was considered a caregiver, looking after her younger brothers and sister. She didn't go to school, as Yousef told me.

One day, when I was taking my sister to school, I met him on our way. He asked me, "Where are you taking your sister?"

"To school," I said.

With a sneer, he said, "My sister doesn't go to school. My father won't let her. He believes a girl doesn't need education. He believes a girl's job is housekeeping, and learning how to raise her children for when she will be married."

When I talked to my mother about what Yousef told me about his sister, my mother said, "Well, Yousef's sister is training very well regarding child care and housekeeping, with having a bunch of brothers and a sister younger than herself."

As I remember the boys, too, quit school as soon as they could, to help their father in the grocery store or to find jobs in other kinds of stores as helpers, or to learn to do something with their hands such as carpentry or welding or ...

I remember very well those days. We didn't have air conditioning at our house, and in summer we had to sleep in our yard. Hajagha Noori's family also slept in their yard, which was much bigger than ours. The thing I remember from those summer nights was the crying of a baby coming from Hajagha Noori's house. Some nights the baby cried nonstop and no one seemed to go to him or her. And that made me frustrated, not only from not having a peaceful sleep in an open area on a summer night, but also being worried about that poor baby, left alone with no care.

Hajagha Noori's name, which was written on the top of his grocery store, was mentioned at our house whenever we needed some groceries. My mother would send me there sometimes for some shopping, such as eggs, yogurt or milk. I didn't like to go there, though. Hajagha Noori didn't treat children kindly. When he saw me, he looked at me with his suspicious eyes and asked me, "Hey, kid, what do you want? Do you have money or are you coming here to steal something?" If Yousef was there, too, he ignored me by turning his back to me as if he didn't know me. At school we weren't friends, either. He was one of those problematic students, fighting with other kids and not caring about his homework.

Anyway, we were still in elementary school when we left the neighbourhood and I didn't see Yousef again until after the revolution.

My father, may his soul be in peace, received a considerable bequest from his own father, and so bought a large piece of land around the Gholhak area in the Tehran suburbs. He built a bungalow with a few rooms, a big kitchen and a big veranda facing the yard. He made a pond in front of the building and put some goldfish in it. A few flowerbeds made the house more pleasant for living. He reserved most of the land for planting fruit trees and vines.

A few years later, when I was in high school, his vines produced grapes and he started to make homemade wine and vinegar. Every year when the trees produced their fruit, my parents invited their siblings and relatives to a party in our garden to celebrate and taste the first harvest of fruits and we had a good time with our cousins and other relatives.

As time went on, Masood, my older brother, was accepted in the faculty of medicine and a few years later it was my turn to participate in the university entrance exam. I didn't dare choose medicine because of the huge number of top students who wanted to be doctors, so I took the exam for the faculty of architecture and I was accepted.

When it was my sister's turn to take the entrance exam, she thought that with her grades she didn't have a chance of being accepted in any faculty. But my father, who really wanted his daughter to have a university education, too, encouraged her to take the entrance exam and to support her, he hired one of Masood's friends to help her prepare for the exam. But Parastoo fell in love with her tutor, or rather I should say, they fell in love with each other. After Parastoo took the exam and wasn't accepted in any college, they were engaged and a few months later they married. A year later Parastoo was pregnant with her first child and her university education was forgotten.

Everything was going smoothly for our family. The orchard trees were growing and producing fruit. In the summer, my father woke up early in the morning and spent a few hours in the garden, taming the trees and flowers. He sometimes came home with a basket of fruits or vegetables. My mother used to tell him, "It seems that you're coming back from heaven's garden." I'll never forget the satisfaction and joy in his face. Mother was happy, too, sewing and knitting dresses for her first grandchild.

But our happiness didn't continue. Masood was arrested by Savak, the intelligence service of the shah. He was in his last year of medical school. After he was arrested we found out that he had been active in a secret leftist group that was against the government; some of them had been arrested and sentenced to death. His arrest was a shock to my parents; a dark cloud covered our family life. Nothing made sense anymore for my parents, not the garden's fruits nor the birth of Parastoo's son, which happened three weeks after Masood's arrest. For weeks my parents were looking for him, searching this and that prison and going to this and that office. Finally they found him in Evin, a notorious prison from which getting out seemed like a dream. Masood had been sentenced to four years; his education was unfinished.

Instead of seeing Masood in his medical office, my parents visited him behind bars and just for a few minutes. But as the wave of the revolution was getting close, Masood was released in the third year of his term along with many other political activists who had been imprisoned during the shah's rule. Masood went back to university to continue his education and again he was one of the activists, promoting the revolution. Unlike three years earlier, he didn't need to act in secret. Our big house became a centre for the activists against the shah.

It was a short time after the revolution that the mosque's mullah set foot in our house. I remember him standing on the veranda, looking at the gardens, the pond with its few goldfish, and the orchard, saying, "This house is a good place for a hossienieh." Which meant a religious centre.

Yousef was among few pasdars who were with the mosque's mullah. As I said, I recognized him at first glance but he pretended not to know me. His behaviour was rude and insulting. He looked at our house like a buyer and said some words under his breath as if my parents had stolen their property from his father.

Three years after the revolution, things changed abruptly. Masood and many of the political activists who were imprisoned during the shah's time were arrested again: some of them were executed within a week. And again my parents were wandering from prisons to revolutionary organizations, looking for Masood. A few weeks after Masood's disappearance, the Revolutionary Guards invaded our house, confiscated all our belongings and sent us away with empty hands. My father's complaint to the legal organization went nowhere. Two months and twelve days after Masood was arrested, his name appeared on one of the government newspapers' lists of dissidents executed in Evin. He had been denied any meeting with my parents, not even a phone call.

However, life went on. I was finally able to finish my education after the reopening of the universities and got a job in the Ministry of Housing and Urban Development. I married Minoo, a relative of one of my friends. She had just graduated from teachers' college. We started our married life in an apartment that Minoo's father gave us as a wedding gift. Azita and Arian were born in that apartment and grew up there. Our life was on track even though we could hardly make ends meet in our household. My father-in-law asked me several times to work in his office for extra income but I wasn't in the mood for extra work or for leaving Minoo alone at home with two small children. In fact, after Masood's execution and the death of my parents, which happened close together, I'd lost all my enthusiasm for making more money and enjoying a better life.

When the children grew up and became involved in social media, they were able to get in touch with their friends who'd immigrated to other countries. Gradually they became interested in immigrating so as to have more chances for a better life and more freedom. It wasn't just Azita and Arian, either. Minoo as well thought of leaving, mostly because of the children. Myself, I hadn't thought about immigrating, even though I had no siblings around to keep me from leaving. My sister had followed her husband to America, with her son and daughter, a year after the revolution. Her husband had gone there a few months before the revolution to continue his education.

The fact was that as time went on, we became lonelier and lonelier. My aunts and uncles mostly had sent their children to Europe, America, Canada, Australia or another part of the world to continue their education and they hadn't come back. Then the children invited their parents and they too stayed away permanently. We suddenly looked around and realized how lonely we'd become in our homeland. In our visiting with these relatives who'd scattered all around the world, and once in a while came back to visit, we got some information about the countries where they lived. So we were encouraged to immigrate, too. We hired a lawyer and filled out the forms for Canada. Meanwhile, Azita didn't pass the entrance exam for engineering and Minoo was worried she might become depressed. But then we received our immigration documents, which looked like the papers of our freedom, and we were able to escape from the trap we were in. Life seemed harder and harder, especially for our children, with the government's tough rules and laws, and also the high rate of unemployment among young people, even those with university degrees.

Minoo was eligible to retire, and I got a one-year leave from my job without pay. So with the money we got from selling some of our carpets and Minoo's and Azita's jewellery we immigrated to Canada, to the city of Toronto, which we'd heard some Iranians call Tehranto, because of its large of Iranian community.

For a year or so, we were able to survive with the money we had. Azita and Arian found minimum-wage jobs for their own expenses. Both of them started university with the help of government loans. Minoo, too, was able to get a job at minimum wage after taking a few courses to upgrade her English. But we still couldn't make ends meet. I tried hard to find a job related to my education and experience but it didn't happen. After a year I went back to Iran and sold the apartment my father-in-law had given us as a wedding gift and sent the money to Minoo. Then I rented the apartment of a friend who also had immigrated to Canada with his family. I had to promise him that I would leave the apartment as soon as he came back.

For five years I couldn't get myself ready to return to Canada, even though whenever I phoned, Minoo and the children asked me to go back. I always made the excuse that when I retired I would come. In this interval I'd been able to buy a small apartment with the help of a government loan and with extra work in a consulting engineering office, and I hoped I could encourage Minoo to come back to Iran. I reasoned that the children had finished their education and settled down: Azita was living with her boyfriend in Montreal and Arian had a job in Toronto and had his own place.

When I heard that Minoo had a work injury, and couldn't work, I applied to retire and went back to Canada.

Minoo had aged much more than I had expected. Azita and Arian seemed like strangers to me. I realized the five years of separation had produced a big gap between my family and myself that wasn't easy to bridge. Minoo had been able to get a one-bedroom rent-geared-to-income apartment for people with disabilities. The apartment had no similarity to the one we had rented when we had just arrived in Canada. I was dejected as I entered the lobby. The carpets there and in the hallways were discoloured and there was an annoying smell that penetrated every corner of the apartment and that made me sick on my first visit. As I looked at the apartment and at Minoo, who seemed alien to me, I blamed myself—not only because I had brought my family to this foreign land but mostly because I had left Minoo alone and gone back to my familiar environment for my own sake.

During the first days and weeks of my return I tried hard to convince Minoo to go back to Iran with me. I reasoned that the children were settled, so staying made no sense for us. In Iran with our pensions and no need to pay rent we could have a relatively comfortable life. Also, I could still find a job and have some extra income if we wanted to travel to Canada to visit the children and they, too, could come to visit.

Minoo didn't want to listen to me. She was suffering from severe pain in her lower back and her joints. She wasn't the same chatty, humorous woman she was before. She didn't like to be far from her children and told me to forget about going back to Iran. Minoo told me that Azita hadn't brought her boyfriend to her mother's place because of the building's poor appearance and location. When Arian wanted to introduce his girlfriend to his mother and sister, he had invited them to a restaurant.

The truth was that my wife and my children believed that what had happened to Minoo was my fault. I had gone back to my homeland and bought an apartment over there instead of staying with Minoo and finding a job here to help the family. I was sure that none of them had any intention of going back to Iran.

I felt guilty as well. The children's refusal to bring their friends to Minoo's place annoyed me. So I decided to stay with Minoo and look for a job. With the help of Arian I prepared a resumé and again with his help I sent it to the recruitment agencies. But as I searched more and looked for a job related to my experience, I found less.

One day when I'd gone to an Iranian store to buy sangak bread, which Minoo liked very much, I met Hadi, whom I knew from Iran. He insisted on giving me a ride to my place. When I asked him to come in, he accepted, but when he noticed my situation, I saw the sympathy in his face. He stayed with us until late at night and we talked about our mutual memories and people whom we knew in Iran and how now they were in Canada, some of them very successful and some not. Among them he mentioned a man who was one of the successful ones although no one knew about his past in Iran. He said there were rumours that he had transferred a huge amount of money from Iran and was now a builder of luxury high rises in Toronto. The man also mostly hires Iranian expertise because he's not educated and can't speak or understand English well. After talking for a while about that lucky person, he imagined that I had a good chance of getting a job in his company as an architect.

For the first time since my second arrival in Toronto I slept with hope and enthusiasm. Then with the help of Azita and Arian I prepared a resumé highlighting my education and my experience in my field. At Minoo's suggestion I gave my address as Arian's. He was living in North York, in one of the buildings that this man's company had built.

The new year holiday was just over when Arian came to visit and brought a letter from the company, an invitation for an interview. The signature on the letter was Jousef Noori. At the time I thought nothing of it.

When I mentioned the name to Minoo, she said, "Yes, he's one of the Iranians who is extremely rich. He receives a greeting card for the Iranian new year from people of power in Toronto." Hearing this from Minoo, I felt a sense of pride that an Iranian had become somebody in this country.

During the days and nights while I was waiting for the interview date God only knows how much time I spent searching the internet for how to have a successful interview. And whenever I talked to Minoo, she mentioned that I shouldn't worry, because of my education and my years working for the Ministry of Housing and Urban Development and also my experience with consulting engineering, and building high rises. She continued, "This gentleman, people say, doesn't have a university education. He might ask you a few simple questions about your job experience."

Hadi, who had encouraged me to send my resumé, advised me to be calm, joking, "There's no ideological test and no questions about your religious beliefs or the number of imams or something like that."

During the two weeks while I was waiting for the interview, everyone pampered me with nice words as if I were going to have major surgery. Azita and Arian talked about their own interview experiences. They advised me to have self-esteem and rely on my education and my experiences. They used the word "self-esteem" so many times that I started to repeat several times a day that I had to have self-esteem.

The interview was in one of the tall buildings on Yonge Street close to Sheppard Avenue, on the thirty-eighth floor. I entered a vast office that faced south to the lake. The secretary was a very young, beautiful girl. I introduced myself and my reason for being there. I waited more than an hour, and when I was out of patience, I told the secretary that if Mr. Noori was busy, I'd come back another day. She went into the office and then came back, telling me, "Mr. Noori asked you to wait," without any apology or reason. I had no choice except to stay. In fact, it wasn't right that when I had a chance to get a good job, after so much anxiety, hope and expectation, I wouldn't let it go. So I sat there and watched the city, which wasn't very clear from that height. Then Mr. Noori informed his secretary he was ready and she sent me in.

I entered a vast room with a huge desk and a black leather chair with a high back. The man sitting behind the desk seemed very little, almost like a dwarf. I was shocked, as if I were watching a bizarre film, but the man's voice brought me back when he called me by my first name.

Hearing my name, which means money in the language of this land, made me think that he knew me, even though I didn't know how. But looking at him for a few seconds, I felt I had an old connection with this man and suddenly I recognized him. He was Yousef Noori, my childhood neighbour and the one who came to our house with the mosque mullah. He invited me to sit down without shaking the hand I stretched toward him. So, rejected, I sat down facing him and for a while I forgot where I was. I stared at his face. He had aged, with salt-and-pepper stubble and hair, and had gained weight. More or less he was like his father, in his grocery store, with a clear arrogance to his gestures. Mesmerized, we looked at each other for a while without speaking but I could read the words from his face, telling me, *Look at me, I'm Yousef, the son of Hajagha Noori, the boy that you didn't like to play with or talk to.*

He made himself busy with the papers on his desk, pretending not to know me, even though he had called me by my first name. But once in a while he glanced at me for a second and then again ignored me. I stared at him whenever he looked at me and I remembered my father when he was forced to evacuate his house and leave behind all his belongings, and my mother's face when she heard the news about Masood being executed.

There was a smile of contempt on his face. I don't know for how long I sat there and stared at that face while my father's words, which he said many times, repeated in my mind: *In our revolution, someone won, someone lost.*

When the secretary's hand was on my shoulder, leading me out of the room, I was still staring at the man and I remembered the day he came to our house with the mosque's mullah and avoided looking in my and my parents' eyes. But I, as an applicant for a job, didn't avoid looking at him. I stared at him till I was out of his office and repeated my father's words: "Someone won, someone lost."

After that day, my family avoided talking about the interview in front of me. I tried hard not only to forget about the interview but also to persuade Minoo to go back to Iran. But in this interval, Azita and Arian had both been married and Azita was expecting her first baby. So Minoo was waiting to see her grandchild.

One day I met one of my friends from the university in an Iranian store. We arranged to meet once in a while. He told me that during his twenty-odd years living in Canada, he had done many jobs and now he was driving a taxi and he was very happy with it. What I heard from him made me think about doing the same.

Now I'm a taxi driver and I usually stop close to the Finch subway station; my passengers are mostly travelling to the small towns in the suburbs that don't have public transit or are far from the bus or subway stations. Driving in those areas isn't tiresome for me, but rather, pleasant. The streets are wide and empty of people and cars. The silence that dominates the houses seems to be the satisfaction and happiness of the residents living in them. When I have to take a passenger to those neighbourhoods, I usually daydream about buying a house for Minoo in one of those neighbourhoods, after working hard for a few years: taking her out of the building we're living in now, which is in the middle of the city's commotion.

On a cold winter day, upon returning to my post, I saw a man standing at the curb of a quiet street. Seeing my taxi, he lifted his hand to flag me. I stopped in front of him. The man put his hand on the handle of the taxi's door, bent and looked at me. Immediately, I recognized Yousef Noori. Hatred flamed in me like an erupting volcano. Without a moment's hesitation, I stepped on the gas and drove away with the car's tires screeching. The street turned to the left abruptly and I drove at high speed, over the limit. After a short while I reached the same spot again and saw the man still standing there. He lifted his hand again, but I passed him without looking at him. I was careful not to drive back the same route. I turned right and entered a vast street that connected to the main intersection. I still had in my mind an image of the man who looked like Yousef Noori. After driving a few more kilometres, I regained myself, and stopped at a curb. I pictured the man's face again and now I doubted that he was Yousef Noori. I asked myself, what would Yousef Noori be doing in that deserted area without a car, in that bone-freezing cold? A flame of shame burned me inside.

And again my father's words resonated in my mind: *Someone won, someone lost.*

THE DAY MY MOTHER BECAME OLD

*P*ARISA HAS RETURNED from Sweden to settle my life as if I'm a teenage boy, can't decide what to do with my life. She says, "Men, no matter, if they are two or seventy years old—they are like children, and need someone to run their lives."

I don't say anything about Parisa's comment. I have no problems with my life. The fact is that I don't want to have a wife and offspring. I'd like to leave this world without any eggs and twigs. What crown did my parents put on their heads with having Parisa and me? Wasn't it because of us that both of them died so young?

Parisa fusses about my life: "You've taken refuge in this run-down old house and are happy with your illusions."

"Do you mean my poetry and my short stories as my illusions?"

In a tone of blame, she continues, "What crown did your poetry and your short stories put on your head? You have a Ph.D. in literature from the best university in this country! Why don't you look for a prestigious job with good pay? Why don't you marry a young and beautiful girl and produce one or two children to fill your quiet house with noise and joy?"

"Did Mother and Father have joy in their lives, were they happy?"

"Why do you talk just about Maman and Baba? Probably it was their fate to die young, but millions of other …"

I don't listen to the rest of her words. Parisa, like millions of other people, thinks "just getting married and having children" means happiness. She doesn't realize that there are children who tie the hands and feet of their parents and kill the love between them. As it is for Afsaneh, I mean my Afsaneh. Her marriage and her children have chained her hands and feet to her family and she has no choice except to stay with them and continue a miserable life. Whenever I tell her, "Leave them and come to live with me. I'm in love with you," she looks at me as if looking at an idiot. I know her reasons. "I can't leave my daughters. Their father doesn't care about them. He'll get married as soon as I leave my home and then my dear daughters would be under the control of a stepmother and their crazy father. They would have a miserable life for sure, and they would blame me for the rest of their lives. I have no choice except to stay with them and protect them at any price."

If Afsaneh didn't have a chain on her feet tying her to her family life, I would have a wife and probably children too. So Parisa wouldn't trouble herself to leave her husband and children in Sweden and come here to fix my life, as she believes.

"I'm worried about you," she repeats once in a while. "Why are you living like a hermit? You look older than your real age. Why don't you marry? Why are you happy with a married woman who has two children?"

Why, why, why? Parisa is full of questions about my life.

She tells me, "You must know if Afsaneh's husband finds out about her relationship with you, what he'll do to her? Don't you live in this Muslim country? Don't you know about Islam's rules and law? Haven't you heard about adultery and stoning to death? Why are you playing a game with that poor woman's life?"

"Afsaneh and I have a good time together, just two hours a week. And that's enough for us. Afsaneh sets aside the chains that have tied her to her undeserved life to be happy and relax with me for just two hours. She—"

Parisa didn't let me finish. "You were crazy since you were a little boy and you still are. The story about the mother getting old in one day was also made by your hallucinations."

After a short pause she changed her tune to be kind and considerate: "Have you ever looked at yourself in the mirror? You've aged so quickly. You don't look like a thirty-year-old young man. Look at me."

I looked at her. At thirty-six Parisa looks twenty-five or even younger. She's happy and full of energy. Her husband in Sweden has an import and export company, and as Parisa says, he's shovelling money.

She looks at me with her eyes full of compassion and says, "You look like a dervish from thousands of years ago. You live in this old, dark house without sunlight and moonlight touching your rooms. You've shut the door of the outside world on yourself, living like a hermit. You live on the small amount of money from renting the second floor. You are happy with a married woman, older than you, with two children. You are young, educated and intelligent. Care about yourself. Your youth won't last forever. There are already white hairs on your head and in your moustache. When you get older, who will take care of you? Ms. Afsaneh? But my dear brother, be sure that since she has her husband and her own children, she won't care about you. And now she's only with you to have more fun and enjoy herself. Those kinds of women …"

I don't listen to the rest of her words. I'm thinking about Afsaneh. When she enters my room, without taking off her manteau or scarf, she throws herself on the couch. There's a tear in her eye but she doesn't let it run. She stares at me with her beautiful eyes and says, "If you knew the hell I'm living in." I don't let her talk about her life in hell, of her bastard husband or her lovely daughters, Laleh and Banafsheh. I don't have anything to do with them. I yearn for Afsaneh—her body and her existence giving life and heat to my lifeless and cold days, or as Parisa says, to my unsettled life.

I ask Afsaneh, "When you marry off your daughters and release your hands and feet from the chain, then will you come and live with me?"

"That's such a nice dream, living with you," Afsaneh answers me with an *ah* coming from her chest. "We have just to dream about it. When I marry off my daughters, the chains on my feet and hands will be stronger and heavier. How can I shame my daughters in front of their husbands by leaving my husband? This is my destiny, to burn and to carry on."

And I remember my mother—the day she suddenly got old. She, too, was tied to her family life, to her children, and was being burnt and carrying on.

I tell Afsaneh, "You're more happy than my mother was. You have me and a place where once a week you can spend a few hours and free yourself of the chain, and so you won't let carrying on burn you up. My mother didn't have such a place to take refuge and because of that she couldn't continue and perished so early."

Parisa says, "Don't bother yourself so much about Maman. That was her fate, not living a long life. Father wasn't guilty of her early death, either. Not all people are supposed to live for eighty or ninety years. One dies young and then some others, late. Father also didn't live long after Mother's death.

"After Mother, Father's existence was of no matter to me."

"Don't be so unfair toward Father," Parisa says accusingly. "Father is dead. You should forgive him. Even though I don't think he was guilty."

"You weren't there and know nothing about how Father behaved toward Mother. I was there."

"You're just imagining things that didn't happen. You're spinning stories. Since your childhood you've lived with your illusions and imagination. It's not for no reason that you write poetry. All is your illusions. But my dear brother, you can't live on your writing. Look around you, and see what is going on. Don't think so much about Mother and Father. Be sure that they wouldn't be happy about your life's situation. Leave this crypt. Buy an apartment in the upper part of the city, where life is going on and flourishing."

"Here isn't a crypt. Here is my parents' house. I was born here. I have lots of memories in this house. I love this house."

"You're really nuts. This was a house years ago. Now it's just a ruin. It doesn't get any sunlight or even moonlight. The second floor, which still gets some sun, you've rented out. And you choose to live like a hermit in these sunless rooms."

"It's not my fault that all the houses in the alley have been destroyed and replaced by high-rise buildings. All of them look to me like monsters, growing from the ground without any memories. These monsters are denying sunlight to me. What's my own fault anyway?"

"I told you, you're nuts. Sell the house and buy an apartment in the upper part of the city; at the hillside, where there are thirty- or forty-storey high-rises. Over there life is flourishing. I'm sure if you live in one of those buildings, you will not only forget Afsaneh's love, but poetry as well. Over there life is breathing and blooming. In this house everything smells of age and weariness."

"Getting old in this house isn't a new process. Since Mother got old in just a twinkle, since that morning when I saw she had become old, the house and its furniture became old as well with the smell of weariness."

Parisa looks at me in surprise, with a mocking smile on her face, and says, "These words won't help you to fix your life. It's years since Mother has been gone and you should forget about her."

"Forget about her? How about Father? It was Father's fault that Mother died so soon. You weren't there and didn't see what happened."

She screams at me, "So, tell me what happened. You just consider Father guilty without any reason. Tell me what happened—I don't know about it."

"Then listen to me carefully." And without letting her open her mouth, I continue, "Do you remember the night when Mother stopped singing? The night that our grandfather, grandmother, and all of our aunts from Mother's side and Father's side with their husbands and children were at our house? And as usual after supper everyone asked Mother to sing. Do you remember what song she sang?"

"Yes, I remember—a love song that was sung by Marzieh."

"Yes, a love song. Almost all songs are love songs. Well, what happened?"

She ridicules me, laughing loudly, as if she had heard some nonsense. She says, "Dear Davood, you weren't even eight years old at that time. How do you remember all of this detail? How did you know of Marzieh? What did you know about a love song?"

Her ridicule and laughter and her doubt about what I'm telling her bother me. I say, "If you don't believe me, I won't say a word."

She begs, "No, tell me. For God's sake tell me. You should talk about everything. Perhaps with your imagination you've made a mountain out of a molehill and made yourself miserable."

"What I remember from that night is running like a film in my head, and I've seen this film over and over. I never talked about it to anyone but I'm sure it's real and it's not my imagination as you say. I had a fear if I revealed it to you or Afsaneh, you wouldn't believe me. Now I feel I have an obligation to talk about it, as if I hear my mother telling me, 'Talk to them. Yes, tell them that you were my only witness for what happened to me. Parisa wasn't there and didn't see what your father did to me. Your father killed me that night. He put his hands on my throat and suffocated my voice. My heavenly voice, as people used to say. Yes, my voice died that night and after that I never sang.'

"Yes, that night, like many other nights when we had a party or were going to a party, my mother sang. My mother had a beautiful voice—as my father used to say, a heavenly voice, and that heavenly voice was the first thing I heard when I opened my eyes in the morning at home. My mother always hummed at home. When I was a little boy, she hummed me childish songs but at parties she sang songs by the famous singers.

"When I became older I heard from friends and families who suggested Father take Mother to the radio station about her voice. They assured Mother that if she took lessons in singing, she'd be a great singer. But Father shook his head and said, 'Parvin's voice is heavenly. It shouldn't be heard by strangers. It's just for her own family.' So my mother sang only at private parties. If there was a stranger among them, she declined to sing.

"That night, we had a family gathering: grandmother, grandfather, our aunts, their husbands and their children. After dinner, as usual they asked my mother to sing. Father tuned his tar and mother sang with her heavenly voice. The group listened in silence. My cousins, who were younger than me, went to the other room to play, but I stayed among the guests to listen to my mother. Her voice enchanted me. My father was right, saying that my mother's voice came from another world—from the world of angels. I remember that my mother's voice mesmerized me. I was totally immersed in her voice when she suddenly stopped singing at my father's hint. And then at his gesture she left the family room and went to their bedroom, which was on the second floor. I followed her soundlessly and hid myself behind the thick curtain. After a few minutes my father entered the room and grabbed my mother's arm and threw her on the bed, slapping her hard on both sides of her face. With each slap I nearly cried out but stifled my voice so they didn't hear me. I peeped through a gap in the curtain and saw my mother had put her hand on her face and was looking into my father's eyes as if she couldn't believe what was going on. His voice trembling with anger, but not loud, so he couldn't be heard outside the room, my father said, 'Now you're singing a love song for that bastard man?'

"The love song that my mother had been singing a few minutes ago came into my mind involuntarily:

> *It's time to go to a desert*
> *And talk to the stones*
> *Take the marble for a witness*
> *For my mad heart*

Yes, it was a love song and very sad.

"Two more slaps came after the first ones. My mother raised her hand to her face again, but she said nothing. Father stayed in the room for a few minutes and then left. I couldn't bear it and started to cry, as if I were the one who had received those slaps. I was consumed by pain. Mother found me behind the curtain. She embraced me, caressing me and repeating, 'My poor boy,' as if she predicted what kind of life was waiting for me.

"I don't remember how long I was in my mother's arms, sobbing. When there were some knocks at the door, she got up, stroked my hair and let me lie on their bed. When she left the bedroom, she assured me, 'Have some rest, I'll be back.'

"I don't know how the party ended that night. And you, Parisa, didn't tell me anything either. I mean, I didn't ask you. Later on I never talked about it. But the day after I woke up in my own bed. That day was a Friday and Father was at home. When I saw Mother, she was old. She was suddenly old."

Parisa says, "This story is just an invention of your imagination. No one becomes old in one night."

Parisa lives in a world of fantasy without a single worry. She doesn't care about the past and doesn't have any worries about her future. Life is like a green grove spread in front of her. She says, "One has to enjoy the moments, because when they are gone, they are gone forever, they're irreversible."

Parisa's philosophy suits her and other people who are around her.

I say, "Mother became old that night and she didn't sing anymore. Do you remember her ever singing again at our family gatherings?"

"Well, maybe she didn't like to sing any longer."

"But I believe since she no longer sang, she became old abruptly."

"You're dreaming again. It might be one of your stories written by yourself."

I've realized talking to Parisa about Mother is useless. I was so optimistic that if I talked to her about Mother getting old, she would believe me. But she doesn't remember that night. I can understand why—she was in love with Jamshid, Aunt Nosrat's son, and was playing the coquette with him.

I tell Parisa, "What happened is that Mother didn't live for more than two years after that night."

"Death won't inform you it's coming. Sometimes it happens suddenly."

"Mother died that night," I tell her. "Since she couldn't sing, she died. Yes, she died. Died, died just because of Father."

Aunt Monir told me the story of Mr. Etemadi's love for Mother. When I tell it to Parisa, she says, "Another story again. Why didn't we know or hear anything about Mr. Etemadi, who married Aunt Nosrat, being in love with Mother?"

"Mr. Etemadi was in love with Mother before she married Father. Aunt Monir told me everything."

"Well, tell me too. I want to know about it. I'm sure you made it up yourself. I've never heard that Aunt Nosrat's husband was Mother's suitor."

"Yes, he was. Aunt Monir told me everything after Mother's death. Before Mother married father, Mr. Etemadi came to ask for Mother's hand. But Mother loved our father, who had a degree in law from France. He was Mother's tutor and they fell in love with each other. But Grandfather decided to give Mother to Mr. Etemadi, who had a considerable amount of wealth. Then when my grandfather found out about my mother's love for my father, who also was wealthy and from a prominent family, he agreed to their marriage. So they declined Mr. Etemadi's hand."

"Why didn't I hear that Mr. Etemadi had been in love with Mother?"

"As I told you, I only heard it from Aunt Monir after Father's death."

"What happened that Mother didn't marry Mr. Etemadi?"

I say to myself, *Not everyone is like you, sacrificing love for wealth and money.*

I say, "Well, Mother was in love with Father. Father also had a good situation. He was a handsome young man. You know that Father had a Ph.D. in law from France and a good job in the Ministry of Justice. Well, they got married. Mother had been singing since she was in high school. She even sang in the school's events. Grandfather said that when she got married her husband could decide whether to make a singer of her or not."

Parisa interrupts me: "What do these words have to do with Mr. Etemadi?"

I continue. "Wait a moment. I'll tell you everything. After Mother and Father got engaged and their marriage was certain, when Mr. Etemadi was totally disappointed about not marrying Mother, he asked for the hand of Grandfather's younger daughter, Nosrat. She wasn't fifteen years old yet. But Mr. Etemadi's huge wealth made my grandfather blind and he gave his younger daughter to Mr. Etemadi."

Parisa interrupts me again, "You're killing me. Tell me the end of the story."

"That is the end of the story. Mr. Etemadi married Aunt Nosrat, so he became one of our close relatives. In two or three years they had a son and a daughter. Jamshid was born before Mother gave birth to you; he was your lover since you were young, as I remember. In short, Mr. Etemadi found a certain place in Grandfather's family and was attending every party and gathering. As I grew up I realized how much Father hated Mr. Etemadi, but he couldn't do anything and couldn't show his hatred—he couldn't send him out of his house. After all, he was his brother-in-law. More than that, he was extremely wealthy and got more attention than other relatives and friends. Don't you remember how many times we went to their villa in Mahmoodabad, or to their Varamin orchard, or in winter to their winter cottage in Dizin?"

"Well, I remember. But what's the relationship between what you're talking about and Mother's death?"

"You don't remember, do you? There was that night when we had a gathering at our house and our aunts and uncles with their families were there too. Then as usual they asked my mother to sing. She sang a song by Marzieh. It was a love song. That night Mr. Etemadi couldn't take his eyes from Mother. Mother, too, looked at him once or twice, maybe involuntarily. It seemed that Mr. Etemadi was mesmerized, staring at Mother. There were even tears in his eyes. Father, too, swung his eyes between them but mostly he fixed his on Mother, as if her voice were emeralds and rubies falling from his own pocket. No one had the right to have any of them. Yes, Father imagined he had complete authority over Mother's voice. Don't you remember whenever someone told him to take Mother to the radio for testing her voice, he answered, no, I won't let this rare, heavenly voice be heard by strangers."

Parisa bursts laughing. She laughs so loudly that I'm startled and ask, "Is there anything funny?"

"It seems you're not living in Iran. Well, this is the way that it always has been. A woman must obey her husband and has no right to do anything without her husband's consent. Father wouldn't let Mother sing for a crowd of strangers. You have to give him credit for letting her sing among friends and family. If Mr. Etemadi had been Mother's husband he might not have let her sing even among her family. Father had studied in France for a few years and as I remember he was moderate and liberal, so—"

I didn't let Parisa continue.

"Yes, he'd lived in France but he killed Mother in a single night. If you were there, you would have witnessed how he slapped her and how he killed singing in her."

Parisa shakes her head, bored, and says, "Leave it. Forget about it—"

I interrupt her: "How? How do I forget that my mother was old in a single night and she died two years after? Mother wasn't herself after that, just full of pain and sorrow. I was there and saw how she broke. Till she died, she never opened her mouth to sing again, not even inside the house just for herself."

Parisa looks at me with compassion and says, "I know it's hard when you think about Mother, but accept that after her death, Father didn't have a life either. He was crushed too. He might have lived just because of you." Then she added, "How many years did Father continue after Mother's death? Eight or nine years? Yes, when I was getting married to Mehrdad, Father told me, 'If it wasn't for Davood, I'd shoot a bullet in my head and end my life.' He was worried for you."

"But his existence or not was the same for me. After Mother, I didn't have a father either."

Parisa raises her voice. "Don't be so cruel, Davood. Whatever Father did, it was because he had too much love for Mother. He told me many times that after Mother's death his life was like a hell. Whatever happened, no one could do anything about it. As folks say, nobody is perfect. I've forgiven Father. You, too, should forgive him."

"What's the use of my forgiveness? He's not alive anymore."

"I'm telling you because of yourself."

"Myself? I don't have a problem, myself."

ADOPTED CHILD

How long can I be a wall
keeping the wind off?
—Sylvia Plath

*W*HAT COULD I HAVE DONE? I didn't believe it, but it was true. He had betrayed me and taken advantage of my trust. I yearned to have a child. I had always wanted to have a child. I wanted to experience my own childhood. You know that I didn't have a real childhood. My mother died very young, when I was only four years old. For years I couldn't believe in my mother's death, which took her away from me forever. Well, to accept the death was not easy, but for me it was worse because I was only a child. And shortly after my mother's death, another woman showed up to replace her. For years I didn't know that my mother committed suicide. Later on, when I was older, my uncle told me the truth about her death.

Well, what could I do? My new mother, or better to say my stepmother, yes, stepmother ...

It's not for nothing that she's called stepmother. She was really a stepmother. Not because she treated me badly but ...

How can I explain? She didn't behave like a mother, her caring had no sign of love, as if she was whispering in my ears, *Get lost, I don't want to see you around.*

As I said, I yearned to be a mother. I wanted to experience motherhood, but I, too, had to be a stepmother. Yes, a stepmother, not a mother.

You know well that I was always busy, busy, busy. Busy with the university, research and trips.

I travelled all around the world. The subject I taught at the university was niche, so whenever there was a conference, I was invited. Not many women worked in that field. I had to do lots of research, had to spend long hours in the lab, behind my microscope, researching and cataloguing.

So I didn't have a chance to have children. Whenever I decided it might be a good time to have a child, a new project, a trip or conference came up and I lost the chance. I planned to have a child and leave my job for a while to spend time with my baby. I didn't want my child to be raised by a nanny or a caregiver. I didn't have my own mother to rely on. My stepmother used to say, I'll take care of your child … and I said to myself, yes, you're right. So you'll treat him or her the same way you treated me.

But I shouldn't be ungrateful. She didn't treat me badly, I'm just not sure she loved me—I don't know. When my father was around, she pretended to love me but …

I should let it go and not talk about the past.

Not having a child has nothing to do with my past and my childhood. No, I wasn't worried about having a child, then killing myself like my mother did and leaving behind a motherless child. No, that wasn't the reason. I told you, the main reason was my job. I always wanted to finish the work I was busy with, then decide. I mean decide about having a child. But when the job was done, there was always another one, a trip, a conference, an invitation to a lecture at universities around the world. Well, they were unique opportunities. I couldn't miss them. I mean, anyone in my situation would have not missed those opportunities.

So that's why it didn't happen. Not that I didn't want to; I always had it in my mind. Always, when I went home, I mean, after a day of work, which sometimes was very long, till late at night, I told myself, if I had a child, poor thing she or he would be in bed by now and couldn't see me. Then I was happy that I didn't have a child. How do I say it? I was happy and sad. You know, a house without children has something missing. In other ways my house had everything. My cleaning lady kept it neat and clean, like a hotel. Well, I wasn't home very often. Hooman also wasn't the kind of man who needed someone to clean after him. He was very organized and neat.

But on Fridays or holidays, in the morning when I opened my eyes, my house was sunk in silence. At those moments it seemed to me someone was asking me, don't you suffer because of this silence? Don't you want to have a child running into your bed and waking you up? Yes, I always had this conversation in my head, as if someone was nagging me and blaming me. But then beside these thoughts there was always work, and the respect and privileges that came with it that very few people were entitled to. The privileges that lots of people, including men, felt jealous of, even toward my husband.

But all these privileges didn't stop me from yearning to have a child. I'm a woman and I couldn't deny my need to have children.

You may think I'm exaggerating. Or perhaps those women have children just because it is part of their nature or part of their way of life, because it is expected of them. As Forough says, *It happens before you think about it*. That's normal. Like having lunch or dinner or taking a bath. So it's a necessity of life to have a child.

But for me it wasn't like that. I waited to have a child not because I had some shortcoming in my life. No, it wasn't that. I loved and respected Hooman. He felt the same way toward me. I'm sure about it. He respected and loved me, too. No, I don't exaggerate. I never felt otherwise. We agreed on everything. Our lives were based on mutual understanding.

When did he betray me? If you call it betrayal, yes, you say it was a betrayal. If it's not betrayal, what was it then? I never found out. I told you, I was busy with work.

Yes, because of my work, I couldn't have a child and postponed it. And postponed it …

And you may say, until you found out that your husband was having an affair. No, I never found out. I did not have a reason to think that my husband was having an affair. He was always with me and still is. Yes, even on the trips. Why not? It was work for me and leisure for him. He has his own business. An agency that his employees could manage it. He had no problem travelling with me. Travelling all around the world was a bonus.

And the child? I didn't know he had a child. How could I know? I was busy with my job. At nights mostly I came home later than he did. No way could I find out that he had spent time with his child. I told you he has his own business, he doesn't have a boss. He can go to work whenever he likes. He probably had enough time to look after his child. I didn't know about it.

When did I find out he had a child? Well, when I was serious about having a child. I was nearly forty years old. I decided to take a leave for one or two years, stay home and take care of my child. Yes, I'd taken a definite decision. But it didn't happen. I mean I found out that it was too late—how can I say, I couldn't bear a child.

Yes, it was hard, it was a shock. Just think about it. In my mind and my dreams there was always a child, a girl or a boy, it didn't matter. I would have loved either boy or girl, a child of my own, my own flesh and blood, a child that I would carry for nine months in my own body, I would feed it and feel its every movement and then I would breastfeed.

Then I found out that I was living with illusions. I couldn't bear a child. Well, what do you think I should have done? My whole body yearned to have a child. My desire was stronger than the academic work I was doing or my grand title or my publications. No, I couldn't continue anymore. I decided to adopt a child. I mean, together with my husband I decided. I mean I had made my decision and Hooman wasn't against me.

When he was sure about my decision, he talked about his own child.

Yes, his own child.

Well, I was shocked. Shock after shock. First to be sterile, then to learn of my husband's child, an eight-year-old girl.

He said, "I have to bring her home."

"What about her mother?" I asked.

"She committed suicide."

"Suicide?"

"Yes, suicide."

"When?"

"After the child was born."

"Who raised the child then?"

"Her grandmother."

"Well?"

"Well, well."

I couldn't say anything.

He said, "Her grandmother has cancer and is going to die soon."

I said nothing. What should I have said?

You mean, I should have asked him how long he had been having an affair. What difference would it have made if I had asked?

But in fact I don't know what to do. This is only a coincidence, a unique coincidence ... Perhaps only for me. Yes, just for me.

You think I shouldn't accept the child but I think the child is a child. She hasn't come into this world by her own wish. If she had the choice, she wouldn't have come. It would be nice if people had a choice before their birth: coming to this world or not. It's funny, isn't it? Yes, it's funny. But this child was born. She has been in this world for eight years and three months without making her own choice and now ...

Do you think I shouldn't accept her?

Should I?

Shouldn't I?

Should I?

NAZLI

*For all those young Iranians, men and women,
who went to the streets, and chanted for freedom in
2008 and 2023*

*Nazli didn't speak
Nazli was a star
She was a bird
She shone for a moment in this darkness and flew away*
—Ahmad Shamloo

SOROR WAS IN THE LIVING ROOM sitting on a chair close to the window, facing the street. The opaque light of the day had been replaced by the glow of the streetlamp hidden among the branches of a stout tree, giving a poetic view from the window. A party was going on in the house across the street. The dancing shadows appeared and disappeared in the window, lit by a delicate light. A lace curtain hung in the window and the sound of music could be heard from a distance. But the vivid sound of a tar, played by Omid on the second floor, reached her clearly—a familiar melody: *Tonight, I have a passion in my head, / Tonight, I have a light in my heart.* But Soror's attention was on the opposite house and she didn't realize when the sound of the tar stopped, even though the song continued to play in her head and nostalgic memories captured her.

Omid appeared in the threshold of the living room, and turned on the lamp. He saw Soror sitting by the window. Approaching her he asked, "Why are you sitting in the dark?"

Wakened from her reverie, Soror said, "Turn the light off, please."

"Why?"

She didn't answer.

Omid turned the light off but he could find his way to the window by the light cast from outside.

Sitting on an armchair close to Soror, he asked, "Are you still waiting for Nazli to call?" And without waiting for Soror to answer, he also asked, "What time is it there right now?"

Soror looked at him absent-mindedly and after a while said, "It might be four in the morning."

"Are you going to sit down here waiting for it to be day there and call your sister?"

Soror didn't answer, absorbed with her own thoughts and the window on the other side of the street.

A car passed and its lights lit the area with a twinkle. Behind the window at the opposite house, people's shadows appeared and disappeared and the sound of Iranian music reached them. Omid looked at the window across the street, too, but as he opened his mouth to say something, the telephone's ring stopped him, breaking the silence inside the house. It was as if Soror were hit by an electric shock. With a jerk, she took the receiver from the table close by, but her voice was subdued as she said hello.

"No, not yet."

...

"Yes, it's possible. But I'll wait."

...

"Sure. When she calls, we'll be there. Don't wait for us, have your supper, please."

"Thanks. Goodbye."

She put the receiver on the table.

"Was it Nastaran?"

"Who else do you expect it to be?"

"Are we going to go to the party or not?"
"I don't know."
"Well, if Nazli calls, she will leave a message for sure."
"But I want to hear her voice."
"Her voice?"
"Yes, her voice."
"You'll hear her voice if she leaves a message."
"I want to talk to her."
"You think if she knows that you're sitting here and waiting for her call, she will call for sure?"

Impatient, Soror said, "There's nothing else I can do."

With suppressed anger, Omid said, "Whoever eats melon has to bear its chill."

"What do you mean?"

"You know very well what I mean. You encouraged her to go to Iran and see her aunts, her cousins and her other relatives."

"I didn't encourage her. You know that she went there because she had an assignment and it was her job."

"But since her childhood, it was you who always talked about her roots. You took her to the Farsi classes and encouraged her to learn, to read and write the language. You read her Farsi books and poems by Forough and Shamloo when she was still a child. It was you, who, if she didn't speak Farsi, wouldn't answer her. It was you who gave her a name from Shamloo's poem, Nazli. Didn't you?"

"Yes, it was me who named her Nazli. I like that name. What was wrong with it? Yes, it was me who wanted Nazli not to forget about her roots and encouraged her to go to Iran. But that was a while ago, when the country wasn't in tumult. And then she got an assignment researching women's issues in the Middle East. She preferred to do it in her own country, her native land. But in this situation, I never encouraged her to go to Iran. It was her own choice. She believed that it was a big chance for her. Wasn't it? You said it when she got it. Didn't you?"

"But I didn't like you naming her Nazli. I knew that Shamloo recited "Nazli" for Vartan, who was tortured and then executed by the shah's government, and since then Vartan has been considered the symbol of resistance and strength for political people. You were aware of all this and called her Nazli anyway, and now you should accept the consequences."

Soror raised her voice suddenly. "Accept what?"

"That it was how you raised her and now she is searching for her roots, for her own name's roots."

"It seems that you don't have any clue of what is going on there. You don't read the news, don't watch television. As if Nazli travelled to Hawaii for her honeymoon."

"No, she hasn't gone on her honeymoon. She's gone to Iran for an assignment. Yes, you're proud that she's working for this and that prestigious newspaper. You are always boasting about her."

"What about you? Don't you boast about her? When you start, you don't want to stop. You're more passionate about her."

"I follow your lead, but I'm always the guilty one."

And then Omid stood up and with anger in his voice cried, "Stop it. Please stop it."

He paced the living and dining room twice, lowered his voice and said, "Let's go to Farhad's party. We'll come back after midnight and you can call Iran when it is daytime over there. She might have gone to one of her aunts' or one of her friends' places and hasn't been able to call. These days communication is not working well over there. And you know that she's not calling us every day. Has she called every day since she's there? Has she?"

"No, she hasn't. But I called Simin to get the news from her. Since yesterday, Simin also has no news from her."

"Well, she might have been in a place where she couldn't call Simin either. I'll go upstairs to change. You, too—let's get ready. It's already nine o'clock. They might be waiting for us to have supper."

He stood by the window, looked across the street, where the shadows were moving. He said, "It seems they are still dancing."

With the telephone ring, Soror jerked again. As she said hello, the words were like pieces of ice coming out of her mouth.

"No, no news yet."

"I'll try. But you'd better have your supper."

"Bye, now."

She put the phone on the table.

Staring at the window on the other side of street, she seemed oblivious to Omid's presence, and as if talking to herself, but actually she was talking to Omid. She said, "Sometimes I wish I was one of them, not just like those ones who are in that party. I mean like an ordinary person who takes pleasure in ordinary things. But me, I don't know why I never have been happy with small things. I'm happy only when Nazli is happy. But she has put me in a situation where I am constantly fearful. Like those days when I was young—in those days, too, I always was jealous of ordinary people, but I couldn't be like them and I wanted to do something but it didn't happen. And now Nazli ... She is following my dreams or your dreams. Yes, happy people don't care about a thing. As folks say, if a flood happened in their houses they wouldn't wake up from their nice sleep. But me ..."

Omid stepped closer to Soror and stood in front of her. With barely concealed anger, he said, "What crown have you put on your head with those fantastic dreams? You aren't different from those people who don't care about a flood. Don't consider yourself in a different class. What do you think other people should do? Hug their knees all the time and be depressed about why things in your country are going the wrong way? You think if you don't care about the world, it will collapse in a twinkle? It has been always the same and it will be the same forever and nothing will change. The world won't bother about your worries. If you show more knowledge about the world's affairs and talk about them, people will be bored and you'll be set aside and have to decay in your loneliness."

Omid stopped talking suddenly, took a deep breath and then continued more feverishly, "I think we have a good life here. We started with nothing and then were able to stand on our own feet. Look at your house. You don't have anything less than your other friends."

Without looking at Omid, Soror said, "We didn't buy this house with the money we made here. We paid for most of it with the money we brought from Iran. The money from all our belongings in Iran, our house, which we bought with the money we made by our work, our carpets, everything that we had there. Don't you remember? When we were new in this country, we couldn't make ends meet. If we hadn't brought money, how would we have been able to make the down payment and buy this house?"

"Well, I know. We have to pay the mortgage to the end of our lives, but still we should be happy and shouldn't separate ourselves from others. Anyway, you were the one who always talked about humanity, yes, humanity. The words that one day you and I wanted to give our lives for. Yes, we didn't do that, but we paid a huge price for it. We were part of humanity as well, or still are, and now our dear Nazli is doing the same as we did when we were young. We might have chosen a wrong way. But I hope Nazli doesn't."

Omid threw himself onto a sofa and with an anger he was trying to control, he said, "And now Nazli, you say, since yesterday you don't have any news from her? Didn't you?"

With a suppressed fury, Soror said, "Yes, it's true. Not once, I said it ten times perhaps."

"You said that your sister doesn't have any news from her either."

He was silent for a while and after a pause, as if weighing his words, he said, "You'd better send the terrible thoughts out of your head. Let's go to Farhad's place. Imagine that Nazli has already called and told us that she's fine. You'll be busy at Farhad's place for a few hours and when we come back, over there it will be day. You can call and get the news from them."

Without taking her eyes from the window, Soror said, "If you like, you can go. Yes, they're waiting for you. If they aren't waiting for you, they are waiting for your tar. I heard you practising. Yes, go and play for them."

"Now you have a problem with me playing tar?"

"What problem? You know very well that I was the one who encouraged you to start again."

"Yes, I know. But it's better to leave these words aside and not keep the others waiting anymore. I can deal with my worries with the tar's melodies. You said you like it too."

"For sure I like it, but not tonight."

"Why not tonight? We've had plenty of nights like tonight. You, or better I say we, raised her like this."

"But I'm always worried about her."

"You're worried about her, but she knows nothing about your worries."

"Both of us raised her like this, caring about humanity, nature and animals."

"But it was you who talked mostly about her roots, about her grandma and grandpa being in jail because of political activity."

Soror interrupted him. "I talked about your parents too. About your sister …"

"Yes, I know, but I wish you hadn't talked about Zohreh."

"You mean she shouldn't know that her young aunt was executed for—"

As if Omid was talking to himself, he said, "Her young aunt who was arrested in the street when she was with her mother and her sister. They threw her in a car and took her away. After two months we found out about her execution through the newspapers and TV. Yes, I think if she didn't know about her aunt's execution it would have been much better. But you talked about her, and when she got the scholarship for studying journalism, you had a big party. Don't you remember? She could have studied engineering, but you told her, with engineering you reach nowhere."

"And you said, with engineering you would serve capitalism and be a slave for big corporations."

With enthusiasm Soror said, "Yes, I'd like her to be a reporter for *National Geographic* and travel all around the world, not to be a journalist for this news agency, which is in service to capitalism. Do you remember how much Nazli loved to travel since she was very young? Why should we force our child to study something that she didn't like? Like yourself, you didn't want to study medicine. You did it because of your parents. And here you didn't continue."

"Yes, I didn't continue because we imagined we would go back to our country soon."

"Yes, because of those hopes I wanted Nazli to learn Farsi. So if we went back to Iran, Nazli would be able to speak the language."

"But we didn't go back. One or two years became four and five and then twenty years and more."

"Well, what's the use of these words?"

"No use, but it's just because you're sitting here and waiting for Nazli to call."

"I have no choice. Do you think I can go among that crowd, dance and sing and listen to jokes? Do you think can I be at ease even for a single minute, not be thinking about Nazli and where she might be? Do you think the devastating thoughts leave me alone, such as she might be shot in the street like Neda or kidnapped like Taraneh, and I will be able to sing with your tar? No, I can't. Believe me, I can't. Do you want me to scream that I can't?"

Omid put his hand on Soror's shoulder, caressing her. Like someone talking to himself he said, "But I am optimistic that Nazli will call and tell us where she is now. Nazli is an intelligent girl. The girl who got a scholarship from one of the best universities in this country knows what to do to not get captured. If she doesn't call tonight, she will do tomorrow for sure. She knows that you and I are worried about her. She's not a child anymore and she knows she's the only hope in our lives. We have told her she wasn't yet one year old when we had to flee from our country at night and cross the mountains. Didn't I tell her that the mountains were all covered with snow and it was possible that she might fall down from your arms into the deep valleys. She knows all about those hardships that we had to endure to come here, to a free country, to raise her in peace, and give her opportunities. I'm sure she's careful and cautious. She will call for sure and tell us everything."

And after a silence that was heavy like lead, in a voice hardly audible, he added, "Even if she was arrested, she would probably call. I'm sure she'll—"

"No, don't say that. I'm hopeful that before dawn she'll call. Since yesterday, I always tell myself I'll be happy tomorrow."

"Tomorrow? What do you mean by tomorrow?"

"I mean, today. I knew that she'd call today and tell us about her return. In yesterday's call she told me that she'd call today and would tell me which flight she'd be back on. Yes, I'm so optimistic that she'll call tomorrow, I mean today."

Omid asked, "Tomorrow?"

And Soror continued, "Yes, tomorrow. Tomorrow is always full of hope for me. And because of that when you wanted to choose a pen name for yourself, I suggested Omid, 'hope.' If I had a son, I'd called him Omid."

Omid gave himself a shake and said, "And because of that you're always hopeful."

"Yes, I'm always hopeful."

"Why then don't you want to go to Nastaran's party?"

"You know why. I'm waiting for Nazli's call."

Omid went toward the window and opened it. There was a cool fall breeze and the sound of joyful and fast rhythmic music coming from the other side of the street. Then the sound of the telephone's ring filled the room.

As Soror was watching the opposite window, where some shadows still were dancing with the music, she lifted the phone.

Note

Neda Aghasoltan was a young girl who was shot dead in the street in 1988.

Taraneh Mosavai was a young girl who was kidnapped in the street, taken away, raped, killed and her body set on fire.

A NICE, OBEDIENT, PIOUS WIFE

A nice, obedient, pious wife
Changes a poor man to a king
—Saadi, an Iranian classic poet

NONE OF US COULD BELIEVE that Bita would leave our gathering so unexpectedly. Well, I believe it was Tooraj's fault, bragging and laughing loudly, telling stories about how he and Bita had got to know each other—the stories he had told us many times in many gatherings. That night Bita was quiet and didn't show any reaction to his behaviour. But after a while, after Tooraj delivered one of those loud laughs, she got up and went to the washroom. I noticed that she was upset and had tears in her eyes. So I imagined she went there to wash them away and regain her composure. When she came out, we tried not to look at her. But then she was standing by the apartment door with her coat on and her purse on her shoulder. I wondered what she was going to do. Our hosts, Azita and Hassan, were dumbfounded. Farzad was looking at a Farsi newspaper, but I don't think he was reading. Bita delivered a short, cold goodbye and left. It was as if all of us had changed to mute people—we didn't say a word. I just couldn't believe that she was leaving. We hadn't dinner yet. It was just a little over an hour since we had arrived at Azita and Hassan's place.

Tooraj froze, his shrewdness and his loud, sarcastic laughter vanished. I'm sure he couldn't believe what was going on. When we realized what was happening I opened the door of the apartment, looked along the hallway, but there was no one there. The elevator had taken Bita to the street.

I returned to my place and sat down. All of us eyed each other, speechless. I looked at Tooraj as if searching for an answer from him. Yes, it was Tooraj's fault, he'd crossed the line imagining Bita as a nice, obedient, pious wife descending from the sky for him. The truth was, from the beginning of their marriage, Tooraj's behaviour had made me worried about their marital life. I tried several times to talk to him about his conduct but I thought he might be getting upset. He is older than me and I imagined he knew what he was doing. It's not my business, but I didn't like the way he acted toward Bita, especially in front of me or his friends. He was the same with Jasmine, but Jasmine didn't take his behaviour seriously and didn't show any reaction to his jokes, which sometimes were insulting. Bita was different. She didn't answer Tooraj's stinging words, but it was clear that she was hurt. Well, this is Tooraj. It seems he has no control of his behaviour.

Azita says, "What do you mean by 'He has no control of his behaviour'? Everybody has control of his or her behaviour."

Yes, Azita is right. But I'm not such a person to say to people what to do or what not to do. Even though now I feel responsible and guilty regarding Tooraj and Bita's relationship. Yes, he was mostly joking, but there's a line for jokes, too. At least I had to tell him to be careful, especially in front of friends and strangers.

Azita says it's women's fault, too. We haven't been taught to be critical toward our family. Especially girls haven't been permitted to speak up in front of our elders. They believed that a girl shouldn't talk too much and always told us to close our mouths. And now even though we are grownups, we still can't express our ideas.

Yes, Azita is right—I feel guilty, too, but not as much as Tooraj is.

When Tooraj came back from Iran and brought Bita as his wife, for me it was like I was growing horns. He still was in his relationship with Jasmine—for more than four years they had lived together. They arranged to go to their homelands to consult their families, they said, then come back, get married and have children.

I mean, mostly Jasmine wanted to have a marital life; when I asked Tooraj about it, he delivered one of those loud laughs and changed the subject. So I couldn't figure out whether he was confirming Jasmine's words or not. All of us guessed that they finally would get married and have children. Jasmine wanted children but not before marrying Tooraj. She believed her child should have a legal father. Tooraj laughed and asked what was the difference between a legal father and an illegal one? Jasmine made a face to Tooraj's question and said nothing. She was a nice girl. I liked her very much and I considered her a good and suitable wife for Tooraj, able to handle him.

When Tooraj and Bita came back from Iran, Jasmine was still in the Philippines. Tooraj said he had come back early so as not to lose his job, but I think it was because he didn't want to lose his apartment, which was in a good neighbourhood, with a reasonable rent. Tooraj never had a permanent job. He mostly works in construction, and honestly I don't know what kind of job he is doing now. In Iran he was a student in civil engineering but he didn't have a chance to finish his education and had to flee the country. And here, he's always was talking about going back to school to finish his education in civil engineering but it hasn't happened.

Tooraj told me getting to know Bita and then marrying her didn't take more than one or or two weeks. Bita isn't talkative. Especially when she'd just arrived, she was a closed person, as if she didn't trust me. I asked Tooraj, "Have you told her about Jasmine?" Tooraj said, "Yes, I did, I told her everything about Jasmine on our wedding night, so she had no choice except to accept it. But she made me promise not see her anymore."

I said, "Why didn't you tell her before your wedding?"

He said, "There was no chance. Everything happened so rapidly. We didn't have a chance to talk to each other and go into the details of our lives."

According to Tooraj, one of his friends introduced Bita to him. He assured him that she was one of those women you can't find among one million women. As our great classic poet Saadi says, "A nice, obedient, pious wife." At twenty, she married a man she loved, a soldier with a degree in engineering fighting in the Iran-Iraq War. But after a month or two, his name had been announced among the missing soldiers. After her husband went missing, Bita didn't go back to her father's house. She found a job and resumed her education, getting a degree in physics. She taught in a high school and declined all suitors, mostly wealthy men who wanted her as a concubine.

Tooraj said, "When Bita was introduced to me, I fell in love with her right then. It wasn't in my control. She was one of those women whom I always looked for: quiet, solemn, understanding and with dignity."

I wished Tooraj behaved toward her as she deserved. From my point of view, Tooraj's behaviour was disrespectful, but I'm not sure whether he did it consciously or unconsciously. His conduct was exactly opposite of what you'd expect from the man who said he so admired her.

He was the same with Jasmine. In her absence, he always praised her proficiency, her liveliness, her intelligence, her caring, but in front of her he humiliated her. I believe he felt deficient and he wanted to compensate for his humiliation by hurting her.

At the beginning of their arrival from Iran, Tooraj's friends and I accepted Bita cordially and invited them to our frequent gatherings so we could get to know Bita better. But because she didn't mix with us easily, as if she felt uncomfortable being among strangers, or felt a big gap between herself and us, we began to ignore her. I figured she might be disappointed with us, or might have had another expectation of Iranians in Canada, assuming we were special people, all educated and understanding. But then it was clear she wasn't happy when she was among us. Even when we talked about Iran and the situation over there, she still said nothing, not talking unless she was asked a direct question. Her answers were short, as if she was saying, *Leave me alone, with your stupid questions*. It seemed to me that she might be a daydreaming person, busy with her own interior world. I wasn't able to get close to her to find out about her family or get some words regarding her life in Iran—the things that we immigrant people do with each other.

Bita kept a distance from us even after a year or two living with Tooraj, and didn't get friendly with any of us. She preferred to be by herself. She probably couldn't trust us. Unlike Jasmine, who became friends with people very quickly, and had friendly relationships with all the women in her workplace. Or when we went to a park together, it was impossible that she wouldn't meet a friend or someone she knew, who would stop to say hello and ask about her family and how she was doing. I'm surprised how Tooraj changed 180 degrees and switched from Jasmine to Bita—two different persons with two different characters. He said he was tired of Jasmine, too noisy. When he had lived with her, he said life with Jasmine never got tedious. She was always full of new ideas. She wouldn't let their lives get boring. And then Jasmine was annoying.

I really couldn't find out how he got rid of Jasmine. I would like very much to have seen her after their separation, but I feel guilty and ashamed of Tooraj's behaviour. And if I were to see her in the street or somewhere, I wouldn't know how to talk her or what she would tell me. If she curses Tooraj and me, I wouldn't be surprised. Anyway, I haven't seen her for the past two years and Tooraj doesn't talk about her either. I don't see any obligation to ask about her. It was a relationship that ended, even though it didn't end nicely. I mean with Tooraj bringing a wife from Iran.

The only element that rescued Tooraj and exempted him from friends' accusations, because of leaving Jasmine, was Bita's character and her behaviour. As I said, at the beginning she was accepted cordially by everyone. She is not only a pretty woman, she has an impressive character as well. She seemed a very knowledgeable and humble person, and her silence and her solemnity impressed all of us and made us cautious about our behaviour in front of her. Later on, we noticed she wasn't interested anymore in our discussions and our points of view, as if she was making fun of us, and that she wouldn't offer her opinion on any subject that we discussed. Then we slowly left her alone. She didn't give any comment until we talked to her directly. One day when she wasn't present, Fariba told Tooraj, "Bita won't stick to us." I think she wanted to say *She doesn't mix with us*, but she used an idiom that was popular among Iranians. Tooraj delivered one of his loud laughs and said, "But she sticks to me very well."

When Tooraj had just come back from Iran with Bita as his wife, his friends were jealous of him, especially those who hadn't been in a relationship. They believed Tooraj was lucky regarding women. In twelve years living in Canada, he had been in relationships with several women and, as people say, each one was better than the last. And the last one was Jasmine, who stayed with Tooraj longest, and because of that we imagined they finally would get married. We all liked Jasmine. She wasn't very pretty, and she was short—she didn't reach Tooraj's shoulder— but she was kind and accepting. She encouraged Tooraj not to drink too much alcohol, especially at our gatherings. When he had a few glasses of whisky, as if he passed his limit, it was hard to stand against him. His loud and frequent laughs and his bragging became annoying. Sometimes I was really worried about him. The only one who could control him and stop him from drinking more was Jasmine.

With Bita, too, he was the same. At the beginning, Bita was annoyed and tried to control him, but then she didn't care about his bragging and being drunk. It was then that I began to worry about their relationship, just a few months after their marriage. Even though Tooraj had told me they fell in love at their first visit, I couldn't believe him. As Tooraj told me, she was one of Tooraj's friend's sisters-in-law and Tooraj had visited her at his friend's house. So his friend arranged for their visit in private so they could get to know each other better. She was thirty-two years old, and as I said before, a war widow.

Yes, Tooraj said, they loved each other and in two weeks they got married. Tooraj was able to arrange bringing her to Canada with him. At the beginning, it was as if Tooraj were flying in the air. He was saying a nice, obedient, pious wife had fallen from the sky for him.

Tooraj is over forty years old and Jasmine was only twenty-four. Whenever Jasmine was insisting on getting married, Tooraj told her, you are still a child and your mouth smells of your mom's milk. If I marry you, my friends will accuse me of being a pederast. I knew that those words were just an excuse. What Tooraj did to Jasmine made me ashamed, even though I imagined he might have a normal life with Bita and I was almost relieved. During the twelve years that Tooraj has been living abroad, he has done nothing positive. He can't stay with any job for a long time and always has been mostly supported by his girlfriends. Jasmine was better than the others. I really liked her and most of us imagined them like a wife and husband.

With Bita, we thought Tooraj's problems would be over. He was able to find a permanent job and for quite a while he behaved like a man of the house. Bita was a newcomer and we supposed because she couldn't speak English well and didn't have Canadian experience, it wasn't easy for her to find a job very quickly. Then we found out that she had no problem understanding and speaking English. Even her pronunciation was much better than that of many of us who had lived in this country for years. She said she had learned English with an American accent online. Her vocabulary was also much better than Tooraj's and mine. She said she always read novels in English and listened to the English-language radio.

A few months after her arrival, she found a job at Hudson's Bay as a salesperson, and after two or three months she got a promotion and worked in the office. From the time of her arrival, she had a plan to pass the English exam for York University and register for a one-year program to qualify to be a teacher. With her experience in teaching high school physics in Iran, she was optimistic that she would a find a teaching job in Canada as well. And I was sure she would do it, and she did in just two years. She is persistent and determined. But alas, Tooraj didn't value her as he might. He sent her away with his nonsense and his stingy language. There's no one around to tell Tooraj, *What's wrong with you? You've married such a nice woman, and as people say, "This woman has descended from the sky for you," you put her in your suitcase, and brought her here. What more do you want? Why couldn't you shut your mouth so as not to hurt her so much until it was more than she could tolerate and she left you.*

After Bita left, I sat down on a sofa and looked at Tooraj, who had a glass of whisky in his hand, and wondered what to say. The laughter was frozen in his face and gradually was replaced by frustration. When he found all of us looking at him, he said, "Did I say something?"

I wanted to tell him, *What more do you want to say? You haven't had anything to say except to hurt the poor woman with your blame and stingy tongue. You either fuss over her dress or her listening to the radio or her reading a book or her silence, saying, She's left her tongue in Iran.* But I couldn't say a word. I just looked at Tooraj and he could read the blame in my eyes. He was really shocked.

Before Bita left, Hassan had said to Tooraj, "Your jokes are like a knife, cutting to the bone." Yes, as he said, he was joking. When Hassan gave him the third glass of whisky, I told him, be careful, Tooraj, you have to drive.

Obviously Tooraj was drunk, his drunkenness was clear from his loud laughter and the way he talked. He said, "Don't worry. Bita drives." And tried to hug Bita but she pulled herself back and looked at him indifferently. Then all of us congratulated her. She answered us with a cold smile, as if telling us it wasn't a big deal.

Tooraj said, "You see, this is a real wife, I mean a nice, obedient, pious wife. This is my golden luck. It's not more than two years since she has arrived here and she has been able to go to university, get a degree in teaching and a good job. Now she has her driver's licence, too."

He emptied his glass of whisky and asked Hassan to refill it for him.

Farzad, who had been quiet until then and hadn't finished one beer yet, making himself busy with an Iranian newspaper, said, "Good for you. Why is there no such wife for me? You are really lucky.

That poor Filipino girl you dragged along with yourself for a few years, promised to marry her, and now you're with Mrs. Bita …"

Then he looked at Bita and said, "Don't give him too much credit. He doesn't deserve you. He's a spoiled mommy's boy, never matured."

I couldn't understand why Farzad humiliated Tooraj in front of us and Bita. It was then that Tooraj exploded with rage and lost control of his tongue. His face flushed by alcohol and his voice coarse with anger, he shouted at Farzad, "You don't need to feel jealousy toward me. You, too, can take a trip to Iran, our beloved country, and bring a wife much better than this one. There are hundreds of them, leftovers of the war's martyrs, all young and pretty, yearning for someone to pull them out from that damned land. You can bring a younger and prettier one. Finding a wife needs some courage and ability that you don't have."

Bita didn't say a word, as if she didn't care what was going on. Then she got up and went to the washroom. All of us were stunned.

Azita finally said, "If I am not mistaken, Bita was insulted."

Tooraj said, "Damn her. Since I married Bita, it's as if she is Queen Elizabeth's daughter. Believe me, she is nobody. If you were there, I mean, in Iran, and witnessed how she begged me with her eyes to take her out from that damn place, you wouldn't judge me like this. We hadn't legally married yet when she submitted herself to me. Don't think that women in Iran are cut from different fabric, pious and untouched. They don't have a pool of water, so it's easy to say they are good swimmers."

Tooraj was talking so loud that I was sure Bita had heard him, if not all of his talking but a part for sure. When she came out from the washroom, she didn't look at anyone. She put on her coat, took her purse, and with a cold and short goodbye, she opened the door of the apartment and left, while Tooraj and all of us were flabbergasted. Then I regained myself and opened the door of the apartment and looked down the hall. There was nobody there.

I told Tooraj to go and bring her back.

He shrugged and said, "Let her go. She doesn't have patience for people. She has been lonely in Iran for so long that she can't tolerate our gathering. Once she told me, 'You waste your time, just talking too much and doing nothing.'"

It was two in the morning when I arrived home and I went to bed directly. But I was awake for a while and thinking about Bita. When Tooraj called, asking, "Is Bita with you?" I looked at the clock close to my bed, it was almost five in the morning. I said, "Isn't she with you?"

He said no and put the receiver down. Again, I was awake for a while and thought about Bita and where she might have gone to spend the night. I was thinking she might have some friends that Tooraj didn't know about, that she might have been with them. But after a while I fell asleep again and woke up to the telephone's ring. The sun was up in the sky and the clock showed 10:20. I recognized Bita's voice and was relieved that she probably had gone home. I was thinking about the previous night and telling myself I should apologize to her because of Tooraj's behaviour when she said, "I'm in a shelter, I just wanted to let you know, and don't look for me."

I wanted to ask her how she had learned about the shelter and how long she was going to stay there, but she said goodbye and hung up.

I remember Tooraj saying, "Bita is a smart woman. If you leave her somewhere unknown to her with her eyes closed, she can find her way and come back home."

I told myself, Bita will find her way. What about you, Tooraj?

LAYLI WITHOUT MAJNOON

The summer heat took away dews
The wind took away tulip's petals
—Nezami Gnjavai, "Layli and Majnoon"

When I was in grade eight, more than half of my classmates were in love. The ones who weren't in love with a real person made up an imaginary one, or were in love with some movie actors. I was in love with our physics teacher, who was a married man but his wife couldn't bear a child. My love for Mr. Radmard, whose first name I didn't even know, as my friends said, was platonic. The thought of marrying him never crossed my mind. Mr. Radmard was the same age as my father. I probably was in love with him partly because I had a good mark in physics and he always encouraged me, and partly because he didn't have a child and I felt pity for him. And also there wasn't any boy around me with whom I might fall in love. All my male cousins were younger than me. The boys who I usually saw in the city square didn't interest to me. I didn't know how they had found out that I was a good student in science and math, and they called me a bookworm. My cousin Shabnam was luckier than me. She was in love with my brother, who was studying medicine in Tehran. Father used to tell me, "You should study medicine, too." He had bought a building in one of the main streets in the city for our future clinics.

Anyway, one of the girls in our class who wasn't in love yet, or she was and we didn't know about her sweetheart, was Layli. Layli was beautiful. Her beauty fascinated us all. We imagined she was waiting for a prince or a very wealthy man who might come from a faraway land and carry her away on his horse. I wasn't a close friend of Layli and so didn't know about her dreams and her life. But Layli's beauty made us dream of being like her. Layli's beauty was unique, I mean unique among our classmates. Almost all of us had black hair and black eyes. A few had brown eyes and light hair, but still looked more or less like the others. Layli's beauty was like a jewel among beads. She didn't have many friends at school because she was from a poor family and never had fine dresses. Some said that her father was a porter in the main bazaar.

Layli had three sisters who were as beautiful as herself, but they weren't old enough to win men's hearts. Layli and her sisters all had green eyes, light skin and blond hair. Sanam, our public baths worker, who was the same worker for Layli, her mother and her sisters, said that the girls looked like their mother.

We lived in the same neighbourhood as Layli's family. Their tiny house was at the beginning of the alley, while ours was at the dead end, with a bigger building and bigger yard.

One night, after we had our dinner, there was talk about Layli's family.

I asked my father, "Is it true that Layli's father is a porter?"

"Well, yes, but being a porter also means having a job. He's not doing anything against the law." And then he continued, "Not that he carries the load on his back. He has a donkey with a cart for carrying the loads."

After that I stayed away from Layli. I didn't like to be friends with someone whose father was a porter with a donkey, carrying loads. Years later when I became older and wiser, and also because of what had happened to Layli, I was ashamed of my earlier feelings toward her.

The story about Layli became public because of Sanam, who came to our place once a month to remove hair from my mother's and Aunt Simin's faces. Sanam told us about Dr. Hoomani asking for Layli's hand in marriage. That night I couldn't sleep till late at night thinking about Layli's life. How she could accept marrying Dr. Hoomani, who was older than her own father?

It was about two months earlier that Farzaneh, Dr. Hoomani's daughter and a classmate of mine, was summoned to the office. She didn't come back to class that day. The day after, we heard that Farzaneh's mother had passed away in childbirth. It was said that Dr. Hoomani had taken his wife to the hospital in the middle of the night and had summoned Dr. Bahrami, a gynecologist who had learned his specialty in France, to his wife's bed. But they hadn't been able to save the mother and the baby.

A week later, when Farzaneh came back to school, she was much different from the happy, talkative and humorous Farzaneh who used to make fun of our teachers whenever she found a chance. As she entered the classroom, she started to scream like an old woman crying for her dying child. She fainted then and was taken to the office. The joyful, active Farzaneh became a withdrawn, depressed girl wearing a black scarf and black socks. And we grade eight students were cautious about not saying anything to remind her of her late mother. But once in a while we would hear her wail either in the class or in a corner of the school playground.

Sanam told us that Dr. Hoomani, with five daughters, had wished for a son. But his wife didn't want to get pregnant again and used to say she felt embarrassed about having a granddaughter and a son-in-law. And when she became pregnant she considered her baby a bell in her coffin, an Iranian proverb for someone who becomes a mother or father at an old age.

It was then that Sanam said, "So it didn't happen as Dr. Hoomani expected. Not only did he not get a boy, he also lost his wife, the mother of his five daughters."

Mother said, "We can't fight with God's will."

"You have three sons and don't know anything about a man who doesn't have one."

"Come on. And this is God's answer."

"But anyway, it didn't turn out bad for Dr. Hoomani. Layli is a gorgeous girl."

"He didn't let his wife's shroud get cold in her grave before he looked for another wife." He quoted the Iranian proverb.

"Men don't care about their wife's shroud. They need a woman to warm their beds."

When Mother was talking of the marriage rumour about Dr. Hoomani, Father sneered silently. He lit his cigarette with the one he was about to extinguish, had a deep drag, sent out the smoke and said, "This is one of those rumours that comes out only from crazy Sanam's sleeve."

Father always called Sanam crazy, saying, "If she had any wits, she wouldn't have left her husband and her child and wouldn't do hair removing for a living."

Mother said, "She had to, because her husband married another woman and left her with nothing."

Anyway, I knew that Father had a great respect for Dr. Hoomani. He talked about Dr. Hoomani's father, who had huge wealth, a respectable man during Ghajar's dynasty. He said that Dr. Hoomani's father was a very wealthy landowner who owned a considerable number of agricultural villages. Even though with the shah's reform and land allotment he lost part of his wealth, he was still extremely rich. My father also repeated another rumour about him: that he was a very self-indulgent man—having a few wives.

After Dr. Hoomani's marriage to Layli, Father dropped the last sentence from his stories about Dr. Hoomani's father, and if Mother reminded him that Dr. Hoomani is a true son of his father, Father just frowned and said nothing.

My mother didn't like Dr. Hoomani's practice: his fee was almost twice as much as other doctors in the city charged. She used to say, "He treats his patients as if they aren't human beings. He doesn't look in their eyes and he's very arrogant."

Father said. "No, it's not right. He studied medicine for ten years. He has a specialty."

If mother answered, "Which field?" He replied, "I don't know. People say so."

When Nasser heard about this, he said, "Dr. Hoomani isn't a specialist. He did the six-year term for general medicine in ten years. He only passed the entrance exam thanks to his father's bribery."

But his office was always full of patients. They might have been attracted by his father's fame, and being visited by Dr. Hoomani was considered a certain kind of prestige. Mother took me once to him when she didn't have any other choice. It was when Dr. Davoodi—our family doctor—had gone to France to earn a specialty. To tell the truth, I was scared of Dr. Hoomani: he was a big man. With his protruding belly, he looked like a pregnant woman, and his big cow-like eyes made me to start to cry. Mother asked him, "Mr. Doctor, what's wrong with her?"

The doctor looked at me as if I were a cockroach. I was ten at that time and very tiny. He said, "She won't die. Be sure about it."

He said it in a way that left me positive I would die. I remember that night: I couldn't sleep because I was afraid if I fell asleep, I might die in my sleep. I cried about my death a few times and also for my mother, who would lose her only daughter. I was angry with my father, who had sent me to Dr. Hoomani. When I woke up, I was so happy that I hadn't died.

Father said, "There's no scarcity of wives for Dr. Hoomani. If he asks for any girl from the prosperous families in this city, they won't reject him. He's a wealthy and well-known man with a good reputation. How can you mean that Dr. Hoomani has no choice except asking for a porter's daughter?

Mother said, "But Layli is beautiful. There are no other girls as beautiful as Layli in this city. Poor thing, if her father had a better job, she would have many lovers for sure. And she had her own Majnoon. So Dr. Hoomani didn't dare ask for her, she is as young as his second daughter."

Father extinguished his cigarette and said, "Don't judge when you're not sure about the facts."

Two weeks later the rumour of the marriage came true and Dr. Hoomani took his fourteen-year-old bride to Shiraz, whose spring was said to have inspired Hafez and Saadi to write those fantastic love poems. Father never blamed Dr. Hoomani, but cursed Mojtaba, Layli's father. He said, "Mojtaba traded his daughter for a shop in the bazaar."

Father glanced at me, but he addressed Mother and said, "How is it possible that a father would trade his own daughter?"

He softened his words and continued, "God helps her to be worthy for Dr. Hoomani. I hope the marriage wasn't by force."

And soothing himself, or supporting Dr. Hoomani, he continued, "Anyway, Layli should be happy with this marriage. This is beyond what could be expected for Mojtaba's daughter."

Since then, once in a while Layli's life was part of discussions at school and at home.

At home, there was Father, who kept talking about Mojtaba, and Sanam, who was going to Dr. Hoomani's household to help Layli. She also did some jobs for Dr. Hoomani's daughter, the married one. She knew Dr. Hoomani's household up and down. She told us that Farzaneh couldn't get along with Layli. They quarreled a few times and Dr. Hoomani sent Farzaneh to live with her grandmother.

When the school was closed for summer holidays, we heard that Farzaneh had been married quietly to her cousin, who was almost thirty years old and had loved Farzaneh since she was a little girl. But Farzaneh didn't love him, the rumour went, and she tried to commit suicide, though she was saved. The news about the suicide remained a rumour, but the news about the marriage was true. It was Sanam who told us that she had done hair removal for Farzaneh's wedding and Farzaneh had told her that she preferred to marry her cousin who was fifteen years older than her than to live with Layli in her father's house.

That summer Nasser sent a message that he wouldn't be home for the summer holidays, because he had got a part-time job in a hospital. Mother and Father and Masood, my younger brother, went to Tehran to see Nasser and also Uncle Ahmad, who had moved to Tehran two years before. Nader and I stayed behind to look after our home. Father said, "Not all of us can to go to Uncle Ahmad's place; he lives in a small rented house." Shabnam stayed with us, too, and our grandfather came to our house in the evening so we weren't alone at night.

Those fifteen days Shabnam and I had a good time, free from Mother's control. Every afternoon, we went to the city square for a promenade and to have an ice cream at Maykhosh, the best ice cream parlour in the city. We sometimes met our classmates and stayed to chat. The city square was a place for young women to find their future husbands, but Shabnam and I went there mostly for fun. Shabnam was happy with her love for Nasser and I hadn't found anyone yet to be in love with and date. I was still happy to love our physics teacher, who was supposed to be our teacher for the next year as well.

It was in the city square that we met Layli again, riding in a droshky along with a five- or six-year-old girl, who supposedly was Dr. Hoomani's youngest daughter. Her droshky was driven by Dr. Hoomani's footman to the main square, then turned around the square a few times. Almost everyone in the square stopped to watch the droshky and Layli, who was wearing a beautiful dress like what we had seen in American movies such as *Gone with the Wind*. In our view she looked like Vivien Leigh, the most beautiful woman we could imagine. Then Sanam told us that the droshky had been abandoned in Dr. Hoomani's father's stable, but Dr. Hoomani repaired it, bought a horse for it and let Layli ride it for fun.

Since that day, we became more enthusiastic about going to the city square, as if we were going to watch a movie star. Sometimes we forgot to have our ice creams, waiting to see Layli. We turned around the square until Layli's droshky was in view on one of the streets. In that time, droshkies had largely been replaced by taxis, and there were only a few of them parked in a corner of the square for giving rides to tourists, and only in the summertime.

Sometimes Layli's droshky arrived when it was almost dark. There were lamps on either side of the droshky and we could see the style and the colour of Layli's dress. For me those dresses were more interesting than Layli herself. Both Shabnam and I believed that Layli's heavy strong makeup didn't suit her childish and innocent face. Shabnam believed that heavy makeup made Layli look like "that kind of woman." Then she explained what she meant.

When Father and Mother came back from their trip after fifteen days, I couldn't go to the square for a daily promenade anymore. But once in a while, after visiting my grandparents, on my return home I would take the longer way and cross the city square so I could see Layli in her droshky riding around the square. People stopped to watch her. Women cursed her under their breath and men were dumbfounded by her beauty and uttered dirty words about her.

The summer was over and I started school again. I didn't have much time to go to the city square in the evenings. Sanam told us that Layli was pregnant and still was riding the droshky in the square. Sanam believed that Layli had lost her wits and was behaving in a way that no married woman does. She believed Layli was playing a game with her own happiness.

Mother, with her face red from hair removal, said, "It's Dr. Hoomani's fault. First of all he shouldn't have married Layli, who is the same age as his own daughter, and when he did, he should have controlled her and kept her at home. This woman is injuring other women's honour."

Sanam concentrated on her work and said, "The poor man! What can he do? As folks say, he's fallen in the pot, craving for halva." She was using a Farsi expression.

I didn't get what she meant and why she called Dr. Hoomani "poor," why she had sympathy for Dr. Hoomani not Layli.

It was winter, and still Layli rode in the droshky in the city square. I didn't see her for a while but I heard from Sanam, who was still coming and going to Dr. Hoomani's place and brought us news about Layli. Layli wanted Sanam to help her with household chores. Sanam said that Layli complained about the maid, who didn't respect her and didn't accept her as the lady of the household. Layli told her secrets to Sanam, talking about her worries to her, but Sanam couldn't keep the worries to herself and she shared them with us.

In the spring Layli's pregnancy was more visible but she hadn't lost her love for riding in the droshky in the city square. She still wore heavy makeup and her hair fell on her shoulders or was piled on top of her head, as some actresses did. With her protruding belly and her eye-catching beauty, many men were either bewitched by her or cursed her because they considered her a blasphemy. But women taunted her and called her ugly names, even though in secret they admired her beauty and wished to be like her.

Once in a while when there was talk about Layli in our home, Father would say, "I'm surprised with Dr. Hoomani. It seems that he has lost his wits completely, with his love for a cheap girl like Layli." And to back up his words, he told us about the love of Sheikh Sanaan, from the story told by the classical Iranian poet Attar Nieshaboori, for a Christian girl, concluding that love is leprosy, and it's incurable. He predicted a catastrophic ending for this love, but he prayed that Layli would get her wits back and become a suitable wife for Dr. Hoomani, who was a respectable man with a good reputation.

My father's description of love made me lose my heavenly image of love as well and Hafez's, Molavi's and Khayam's love poetry became meaningless for me.

Layli's death in childbirth was a shock to me and I decided I would never fall in love and never get married. My love for our physics teacher faded away too.

Sanam told us the story of Layli's death in details that stayed with me for years and once in a while appeared in my nightmares— screaming, and Dr. Hoomani with a knife in his hand, tearing apart Layli's belly and taking out a freak baby with a huge head, then Dr. Hoomani laughing like a lunatic. I would wake up wet with my sweat and scared as if all I had dreamed was real.

Sanam had said, "Dr. Hoomani wouldn't agree to bringing in any doctors to help Layli deliver her baby. And the head of the baby was so big that Layli couldn't have a natural delivery. Dr. Hoomani did a caesarean section on Layli in his own clinic, which wasn't suitable for this kind of operation." Then she continued, "What a head. Big as a grown man's, with an old face. God forbid any woman giving birth to such a baby. A real freak."

The images that Sanam drew for us of Layli's childbirth and her baby were so frightening. Mother couldn't hide her fear either and said, "It was God's anger. God knows what to do to punish his sinful slaves." Then with sympathy she added, "The poor girl." The same one who was a prime example of sin till just a few days ago.

Since then it was Layli who was the subject of sympathy; even Father, who had always blamed Layli sometimes said, "It was her stupid father's fault. He traded his young daughter for a booth in the bazaar and now he has to mourn for the rest of his life. I hope he has become wiser regarding his other daughters and won't trade them too."

As usual, sad and happy stories finally are forgotten as time goes by, and so Layli's story also faded away. A few months later Sanam told us that Dr. Hoomani had married again, this time to a divorced woman who couldn't bear a child. As she was still coming and going to Dr. Hoomani's place, she was still the source of news about his household. We heard from her that Layli's son was taken care of by a rural woman whom Dr. Hoomani brought from his village, and was fed cow's milk. With pity, she told us that none of Dr. Hoomani's family members cared about Layli's child.

Father said, "It's still good that Dr. Hoomani didn't send him away, as Saam in the Shahnameh did with his son Zaal who was abandoned in the mountains and was raised by a phoenix." This was from a tale told by Shabnami in the ninth century.

I finished high school and moved to Tehran to study medicine, as my parents wished. I got my specialty in pediatrics and came back to our city; I had my clinic in the same building where my brother was.

Layli and her dramatic life had vanished from people's memories. There was no news about her sisters either. They might not have had a story like their sister Layli.

One day when I was passing Dr. Hoomani's clinic, which was still in the same location, I saw a dwarf sitting on the doorstep. He had a big head, which attracted my attention—I looked at him with curiosity.

That night, when I talked to my parents about the dwarf on Dr. Hoomani's clinic's steps, my mother said, "He's Dr. Hoomani's son. And after a while she continued, "Layli's son. Don't you remember Layli, who died in childbirth?"

"So Dr. Hoomani finally got a son?"

Father said, "Whoever eats melon has to bear its chill."

Mother said, "But Dr. Hoomani ate a very expensive melon. And it was Layli who got the chill and lost her life."

Layli's painful story reminded me that almost all of my classmates had envied her and wished to be as beautiful as she was. Even though Layli's beauty was fascinating and unique, I wondered why she hadn't had a lover like the Layli in Nizami Ganjavi's story of Layli and Majnoon.

As if my Mother had read my mind, she said, "Did you know that Layli's cousin was in love with her? And when Layli died in childbirth, her cousin became so depressed that he committed suicide a few months later."

I was so shocked I didn't say a word. It seemed that all Laylis and Majnoons around the world have had the same story.

Note

"Layla and Majnun" (English: "Possessed by Madness for Layla"; Arabic: مجنون لیلی; [*Majnun Layla*]) is a love story that originated as a poem in eleventh-century Arabia, and was later adapted by the Persian poet Nizami Ganjavi as "Layli and Majnoon." (Source: Wikipedia)

ZIBA SEPIDROOY

The first day Zinat came to my place to clean, there was a four- or five-year-old girl with her.
She said, "Don't worry, she won't bother you."
I asked her, "What's her name?"
"Ziba."
With a sneer, she continued, "Her name is Ziba, but she isn't beautiful. Her family name is Sepidrooy, but as you see she's neither beautiful nor white."
In the girl's face was a hidden sadness, the sadness of not being beautiful, perhaps. But she was beautiful; like children all around the world, she was beautiful.

I gave her a doll. She took it with reluctance. In her eyes was the same hidden sadness. It seemed that the doll didn't make her happy.
Zinat asked, "Why is the doll black?"
"Well, it's black anyway."
"Like Ziba." And she laughed sarcastically.
I said, "The doll is beautiful, like Ziba."
And Ziba stared at the doll with the same sadness.

Ziba was sitting in a corner, playing with her doll.
I said, "Zinat, it's time for you to have one more child."

"No, for me, one is enough. Our shah says, 'Fewer children, a better life.'"

"Two is not many. Think about Ziba; a sister or a brother …"

Ziba looked at her mother, then at me and put her head down. She caressed her doll's hair.

I said, "Ziba is a clever girl."

"What do you mean by clever? I wish she was beautiful. I could marry her off. But …"

In her "but" was regret and in Ziba's eyes was sadness.

I put some money inside a sketchbook and gave it to her along with a box of coloured pencils.

Zinat grabbed the sketchbook from her and took the money, saying, "Children don't need money."

I said, "Buy her a new dress."

"She's ugly. Even wearing velvet, still she's ugly."

Ziba gave me the sketchbook and said, "It's for you."

I went through the pages. It was filled with sketches. A little girl with a sad face beside a flower bed or in a corner of a yard—lonely, by herself.

I said, "Ziba, your sketches are beautiful, like you." A sad smile appeared on her face. The next week I gave her another sketchbook with another box of coloured pencils. And again she filled it with her pictures of flowers and birds, and gave it to me the week after when she came to my place with her mother.

After a year, Zinat arrived with a baby in her arms and Ziba.

I said, "What happened?"

"Imam says there is a need for more soldiers for Islam's army."

Ziba was sitting in a corner and cradling Maysam on her legs. She was sketching the table, chair, TV or whatever was around her. Her mother screamed at her, "Leave that sketchbook aside and take the child outside."

Ziba took Maysam in her arms and went to the yard.

I said, "Zinat, Ziba is a good girl. Why are you mad at her?"

"She doesn't help me. She just wants to do drawing."

"She likes to draw. You don't let her play with her doll. You believe it's sinful, and she has to give life to the doll in the doomsday. So she shouldn't draw? You weren't always so superstitious."

"She's committing a sin. I have to marry her off."

"Marry her off? She's only ten years old."

"The girls become mature at ten."

"But you? Weren't you miserable marrying so young?"

"It was my fate."

I gave Ziba a box of watercolours and a big sketchbook and told her, "This is your gift for the new year."

She took them with the same depressing smile and said, "I'm the first student in my class."

"Good for you. Keep studying hard. You must become someone."

"Talk to my mother, please."

Zinat came to my place with two children and Ziba. One was in Ziba's arms and one in hers.

I asked her, "Isn't your husband working?"

"He's working for the Masjid's imam."

"He's not working in construction anymore?"

"No, he gets a wage from the imam."

"Doesn't he give you money for home?"

"He married another woman, a widow of the victims of the war."

Ziba gave me the sketchbook and said, "It's for you."

I looked at it. Half of it was blank.

I asked, "Why didn't you complete it?"

Zinat said, "Next week she's going to her husband's home."

After Ziba married, I didn't see Zinat anymore. She invited me to Ziba's wedding but I didn't go and I didn't want Zinat to come to my place for cleaning any longer. Then we immigrated to Canada and I didn't find out what happened to Ziba.

Taraneh said, "Look. Most of the features look like you."

"Me?"

"Yes, you. Look closely. It's as if the painter was painting your face."

I said, "I don't know the painter," as if Ziba Sepidrooy was a name I had never heard.

I asked the gallery director about the painter. She said, "She was supposed to show up but something happened and she couldn't make it."

The gallery was full and the paintings were very expensive.

Taraneh said, "Look at this. It's exactly you. A young woman caressing the head of a five- or six-year-old girl." The little girl's face wasn't clear in the painting.

A man got close to the painting and asked the gallery director the price. The director said, "It's not for sale."

The man said, "It's a masterpiece. I'll buy it at any price."

I looked at the painting. Was she me or a woman who looked like me?

My doorbell rang and I went to answer it. I saw a van in the parking lot. The man who rang the bell asked me, "Are you Simin Bahrami?"

"Yes, it's me," I said.

"Ms. Sepidrooy has sent a painting for you. Will you let me bring it in?"

"Why not?" I said.

And I said to myself, why me?

The man brought the painting and asked me, "Where do I leave it?"

I showed him a place in the living room. He put the painting against the wall, gave me a package and left.

I removed the paper from the painting. It was the same woman and the little child, the painting that didn't have a price in the gallery, the one a buyer was ready to pay any price for.

Was I the woman in the painting?

I was absorbed in looking at the painting and confused. I wished Taraneh was there, too, to see that the painter had given the painting to me. But why me? I opened the package. It was a sketchbook and a letter. I read the letter first.

Dear Ms. Simin:

Anything I have is because of you, from those sketchbooks and coloured pencils that you gave me when I was a little girl. My small gift to you is just to say thank you. All these past years, you were in my mind and this sketchbook is the same one that I wanted to give you but you said, keep it. I kept it for you.

With love and appreciation,
Ziba

I paged through the sketchbook. It was full of drawings of a ten-year-old girl, from all around our house in Iran. Paintings of me, my daughter, Azita, my son, Nima, and my husband, Farhang. That day I gave the sketchbook back to her. Half of it was blank then. Remembering that day, I felt regret, and recalled a blackish girl who had an unsaid sadness in her eyes.

I searched her name in Google and found her in Wikipedia.

Ziba Sepidrooy, born in Hamadan. Married at eleven years old. Widowed at fifteen, with a daughter called Simin; her husband was killed in the war.

At twenty-one, she got her high school diploma, then a bachelor's degree in fine arts from the University of Tehran. She was awarded a scholarship in England.

The names of the cities and countries in which she has had exhibitions haven't stayed with me.

I called the gallery. A woman answered the phone. I asked about Ms. Sepidrooy.

She said, "She left Toronto at the end of the exhibition."

I asked her, "Do you have any address for her?"

She said, "No."

A SUMMER'S AFTERNOON

THERE WAS THE NOISE of the door of the house opening and closing and then the sound of feet running up the stairs.

"Why are you sitting here?"

The woman was sitting on the edge of the bed in the bedroom. She didn't answer.

"I saw your friend."

The woman said nothing, staring at nowhere.

"Ms. Mahboobeh was crossing the street."

The woman looked at the man and asked, "Did you talk to her?"

"Yes, I did. She'd come to our door to go to the park with you, but she said you weren't home. Were you?"

The woman said nothing, stood up, and left the room.

In the family room, she sat on the sofa. The TV was on and the show was halfway over. She looked at the TV for a while, without paying attention to the program. She turned the TV off, went to the deck and sat down on a bench. A bird, singing a melancholy song, reminded her of the coming fall with its cold, windy short days. She didn't know the name of the bird and always tried to find it among the branches but wasn't able to. A breeze passed through the leaves, whispering a sad story from the coming night.

Hearing the ring of the doorbell, she'd climbed the stairs up to the second floor and from the window looked to the street for who was there. When she saw Mahboobeh, she stood back so that if Mahboobeh lifted her head, she couldn't see her. She wasn't in a mood to go out with her. Mahboobeh rang the bell twice, then left after a while.

The man came to the yard, wearing shorts and a T-shirt. He took the hose from the hook on the wall, turned the valve on and started to water the flower beds.

When the man got close to the veranda, the woman said, "Mahboobeh didn't say what she wanted?"

"No, she didn't. She said she was going to the park."

The woman didn't ask more.

While watering the flower beds, the man looked at the woman and said, "Why didn't you go to the park with Mahboobeh?"

The sound of water flowing on the flower beds and the lawn filled the area. The bird was still among the branches and singing in its melancholy way once in a while.

The woman listened to the water and the bird's song for a while. The man was at the other side of the yard, busy watering the flowers. The sunlight lit a corner of the yard and the highest branches of the trees.

The woman went inside the building, then came back to the veranda dressed for outside. The man turned and looked at her.

"Where are you going?"

"I'll go for a short walk and come back soon."

In the park, she looked for Mahboobeh in the area where they spent time together, and after a while she found her sitting on a bench. The sun's rays were casting light and shadow on her and reminded the woman of "A Clean, Well-Lighted Place" by Hemingway, one of Mahboobeh's favourite short stories. The question of whether Mahboobeh was happy crossed her mind. No, she wasn't. Yes, she was.

She didn't realize how long she stayed there watching Mahboobeh, who used to say she was getting out of her lightless room to be with the trees and birds.

When Mahboobeh stood up and was lost like a shadow among the trees, the woman realized that the sun had almost set and she hadn't moved from the spot where she was standing and watching Mahboobeh. Then she walked through the trails that she had usually walked with Mahboobeh. Rays of sunlight still lit the highest branches. She suddenly met Mahboobeh at a curve. Mahboobeh was surprised to see her, and asked, "Were you in the park too?"

The woman said nothing.

"I was walking back home."

"Bahram said he'd seen you in the street and you told him you'd come to see me and I wasn't home."

"Were you?"

"Yes, I was." And she waited for Mahboobeh to ask, *Why didn't you answer the bell?*

Instead, Mahboobeh asked, "Why are you sad?"

"Sad?" And after a while she asked Mahboobeh, "Are you happy?"

"Happy?" Mahboobeh looked at her for a while, then with a tone of mockery in her voice said, "Sometimes."

The woman said nothing, looking at Mahboobeh in a forlorn way. Mahboobeh asked, "Would you like to be in my place?"

The woman looked at Mahboobeh and said, "Sometimes."

Leaving the park, they said goodbye and went their separate ways. The woman was thinking about what she had said to Mahboobeh. *It was good I didn't lie to her.*

But in fact, she had lied to her. She had never wished to be in Mahboobeh's place, even though she was jealous of her and didn't feel happy in her own place either.

SADIKA

Homayoon opened the door with his key and entered the apartment. Zari was paging through one of the Iranian newspapers without being interested in reading any article. She lifted her head toward the door and looked at Homayoon. She couldn't read anything in his face, not the bitterness of failure nor the sweetness of victory. Homayoon closed the door, looked at Zari, then peered around and asked, "Where is Goli?"

Ignoring Homayoon's question, Zari said, "What happened?"

Homayoon took off his coat, hung it in the closet, looked through Goli's room, then stood in front of Zari and inquired, "What have you done with Goli?" Zari folded the newspaper, put it on the table in front of her, sat upright and said, "What do you mean by 'What have you done with Goli?' Goli is with Sanaz, at Mahnaz's place."

Homayoon threw himself on the sofa and breathed deeply. The TV was off and the potted plant with its large green leaves beside the TV tilted toward the window, as if it was tired of standing in the same spot. Homayoon looked at his hands and chewed his nails. His belly tightened in his new grey shirt and his white-and-red-striped tie was askew on his chest.

The curtains were pulled aside and a gloomy sky filled the window. Homayoon looked at the sky, then he turned toward Zari, who was sitting on the other side of the sofa, and said, "Didn't I tell you a thousand times not to send my daughter to Mahnaz's place?" Pronouncing "Mahnaz," he screwed up his mouth as if he was ridiculing her.

Zari didn't take her eyes from him. "Did they accept you or not?" Homayoon looked at his hands and turned the wedding ring on his finger several times. He had put the ring on his finger that morning, before going out. Then he took it off, breathed deeply and threw it on the table in front of the sofa. Zari made her voice louder and more persistent, asking, "You're killing me. Tell me what happened."

Without looking at her, Homayoon said, "Since you haven't brought my daughter back, I won't say a word."

Zari made her voice louder still and said, "The sky won't collapse if she stays there for a few minutes." And she turned her eyes from him, continuing, "What is wrong with you, repeating my daughter, my daughter?"

Homayoon, still looking at his fingers, then sat upright and said, "Yes, the sky will collapse. I told you a thousand times that I don't like my daughter mingling with that woman who is morally worthless and loose …"

Zari interrupted him and said, "Well, well, don't be so fanatical," and looked at Homayoon. He turned toward her and their eyes met. Zari said, "You've failed again …?"

Homayoon said, "I didn't fail. I didn't accept the job." And there was a smile on his face that wasn't clear. Was it a sign of regret or arrogance?

Zari turned ninety degrees toward him and said, "You didn't accept the job? A good job like that …?" She couldn't say anything more.

Homayoon closed and opened his fingers several times. He was looking out the window. From his perspective he could see nothing except a grey sky and the curtains that framed the sky.

Zari stood up and walked toward the window, which wasn't more than a few steps, and turned back. She stood a distance of two steps in front of Homayoon and said, "Why? Why didn't you accept the job, Mr. Doc—"

Homayoon stared at her for a few minutes. There was an inscrutable smile on his face that made Zari more disturbed.

"Can you explain what you're smiling at? Haven't you been accepted or didn't you accept the job? That was a job you looked for so eagerly, for so long, and we needed it so urgently. Perhaps you are waiting to get a proposal to be the head of Mount Sinai—" She cut her words short and stared at Homayoon. She tried to control herself and went on. "But you'd been accepted in the first interview."

Before, Homayoon had told Zari that he would prefer to get a job at Mount Sinai hospital rather than at other hospitals.

Homayoon said, "Yes, I didn't accept it. If you were in my place neither would you."

Zari sat on the sofa close to Homayoon and asked, "Why not? Why, if it was me, wouldn't I accept it? I can't understand."

Hamayoon, still staring at the grey sky spread out behind the window, said, "Yes, as I said, if it was you, you wouldn't accept it either."

He gave himself a shake and looked at Zari and said, "How many times have I told you, don't send my daughter—"

Zari interrupted him: "Again, the same subject."

"How do you do that? My daughter still can't recognize her left hand from the right one. You would like to raise her like your friend?"

Zari said, "The child was lonely, I sent her to be—"

Homayoon interrupted her, "Keep your reasons for yourself. Go and get the child back."

Zari put her hand on Homayoon's leg, which his pants looked too tight for, and said, "Since you haven't told me why you didn't accept the job and that if it was me I wouldn't accept it either ..." Then she changed the tone of her voice and said, "You know, it's better Goli stays with Sanaz and doesn't listen to our argument. My poor child was happy that her baba had gone to an interview and would be back with a box of pastry."

"You told her that I'd gone for an interview?"

"I didn't. But she knew about it. During these past few days, was there any talk between us except about your interview?"

Homayoon looked at Zari and said, "I think it is only Khajeh Hafez Shirazi who hadn't heard about my interview."

Zari smiled and said, "Khajeh Hafez was the first person who heard about your interview. Have you forgotten that you first asked Hafez's divination?"

And Homayoon said, "Yes, I remember."

"Well, now tell me why didn't you accept the job and why if it was me, I wouldn't either."

Homayoon took the wedding ring from the table and looked at it, then looked at Zari and said, "If I tell you who was supposed to interview me, you'll not only not believe me, you may grow a horn on your head."

Zari asked, "Who?"

Homayoon put the ring on his finger and again took it off and said, "Sadigheh. Here she is called Sadika."

Zari sat a little farther back, and with wonder in her eyes she asked, "Sadigheh? Sadigheh Najarzadeh. That butterfingers, that arrogant woman? The one who didn't know her left hand from the right one when she was a newcomer here? The one who always talked about going to university and getting a Ph.D."

And after a while she asked, "What is she doing here?"

Homayoon looked at Zari and smiled, and with a mocking laugh said, "Her secretary called her Ms. Doctor."

Zari said, "But when she came here she had only a bachelor's degree. What kind of bachelor's, I don't remember. Social science or something. She looked for any kind of work, and couldn't get a job until you gave her one in that Iranian community centre. When did she become a doctor?"

Homayoon said, "Not a doctor."

Zari said, "What then?"

"I don't know. Leave me alone. And you imagine that I could work with such a person? Is it possible? Look at me."

Zari sighed deeply and said, "And you, a psychotherapist with your degree and so many years of experience practising as a physician, should—"

Homayoon leaned his head on the back of the sofa and said, "Yes, one day I was a doctor, but now ..."

Zari said sympathetically, "What kind of doctor is she? Is it so easy to become a doctor in this country? When you looked into it, there was a big barrier and everyone said that it was impossible for you to practise as a psychotherapist in Toronto." She asked, "Does she have an office, too?"

Homayoon looked at Zari and laughed disdainfully, then with contempt said, "Did you imagine she had become a physician?"

With a question in her eyes, Zari asked, "Then what?"

"Maybe a psychologist."

"Psychologist?"

"Yes, I think so."

"Like you?"

"Not like me. I'm a psychotherapist. I mean, I was, and here—"

Zari didn't let him to continue. "You mean you should work under her command? What kind of work would you be supposed to do? Be her secretary?"

"Leave me alone. You make me tired."

Zari sounded pitying as she said, "You made the right decision. Working under Sadigheh Najarzadeh? That would be a shame. Do you remember her father in Iran? A security guard in our building? He had six daughters and none of them could find a husband. Sadigheh was saying that six of them left Iran. Two of them are in the U.S., two of them here and two of them are in Sweden. They have spread all around the world. So she was busy getting a degree and becoming a doctor and getting—"

Homayoon interrupted her and said, "And you expected me to work under a person like Ms. Sadigheh?"

Zari asked with caution, "You mean she accepted you but you didn't take the job?"

"No, I didn't even accept to be interviewed. When I saw her sitting behind that desk like a big bus, I just fled from there. I've taken all kinds of humiliation in the past few years, except this one, that the daughter of Mostafa the security guard of our building would be my boss? I told myself, no, not me."

Staring at the grey and gloomy sky outside the window, following Homayoon's story, Zari said. "No, me neither. If it was me, I wouldn't accept it. But …"

"But what? I couldn't do it."

"No, you shouldn't. Sadigheh …"

She breathed deeply and said, "You working for Sadigheh, the daughter of Mostafa the security guard?"

In confirmation of Zari's words, Homayoon said, "We are from the original families in Iran. We weren't like—"

Zari continued, "You are right. But here a family's origin counts for nothing. Anyone with no family at all can get a high-level job and interview a person like you, with your degrees from England and France, your job experience and your prestigious background." She stopped talking, as if she was tired, and after a pause said, "But who has interviewed her?"

Homayoon said, "And who has given her that high-level job and that prestige? No, I can't take it. I didn't even enter her room. Her secretary followed me to the top of the stairs and called me. Running down the stairs, I cursed her and her boss and left."

"Did you curse her loudly?"

"No, I wasn't so stupid as to make problems for myself."

Zari was quiet, but the silence didn't last long, as if the quiet made the misery heavier.

She said, "This is just a bad luck. If you had gotten the job …"

"Yes, if I'd gotten the job, it wasn't a bad job, related to my education and my experience, psychotherapy. I would have had more chance to be accepted later as a physician."

Zari repeated, "Just bad luck."

"What do you mean by 'bad luck'?"

"It was just bad luck, as you said. If only someone else, another Sadigheh, from another country, could have interviewed you."

Homayoon asked, "For example, who?"

"How should I know? From another country, a Chinese, a Bangladeshi or whatever. Another Sadigheh from another country.

If she wasn't our fellow countrywoman and the daughter of our building's security guard in Iran."

Homayoon said, "Yes, if she was someone else, another Sadigheh from another part of the world, I would have accepted the interview and the job. But it was my bad luck that Ms. Sadigheh should interview me. If I had known that Sadika was the same as Sadigheh, I wouldn't have applied for the job."

The door of the apartment opened and Goli, followed by Sanaz, came in. The little girl threw herself into her father's arms and asked, "Baba, did you buy pastry? Sanaz is here to eat sweets."

Zari asked, "Did you tell Mahnaz that you are here?"

Sanaz said, "Maman went out with Uncle Bahram and told me to stay with you until she's back."

The early autumn night dominated the apartment. Zari had left Goli in her bed. After she asked a few times for sweets, finally Homayoon had to yell at her to stop it and the child had fallen asleep crying. In the bedroom, Homayoon snoozed without a blanket covering him. Zari was sitting on the sofa in the living room. The TV was off and there was no sound in the apartment except the buzz of the refrigerator. The dark, starless sky was visible out the window. A silent, melancholy atmosphere dominated. A lamp with a long base beside the sofa spread a weak light around the area where Zari was sitting. When the sharp ring of the telephone filled the room, Zari jerked in her place and picked up the receiver quickly so as not to wake Goli.

"Ms. Zari? It's me, Sadika. Remember me?"

"No."

"Sadigheh. Sadigheh Najarzadeh. Here they call me Sadika. Like you that in Iran were called Zahra and here Zari."

Zari wanted to say, *In Iran, too, I was Zari.* But Sadika said, "How is Mr. Doctor?"

Zari said, "Doctor is good and says hello." But she was angry with herself for saying so.

Sadika said, "I wanted to talk to him about today. I wanted to apologize to him. There was an urgent task and I had to leave the office. But the job is there. In fact, if I had done the first interview, I would have told him that he's accepted. But the whole day I had a conference at the university. If Mr. Doctor accepts the job, he can come tomorrow or the day after and sign the contract. I know that the job is much lower than the level of his education and his experience, but you know very well how things work here."

Joy filled Zari and she said, "Yes, I know."

Sadigheh continued, "In fact, today I talked to my father—my father is here, too, you know. He is very interested to see you and Mr. Doctor. He suggested that we should hire Mr. Doctor. I can understand what situation you are in. Immigration is not that easy, especially for a person like Mr. Doctor, and how Canada won't accept our degrees no matter what we have achieved in our homeland ..."

Zari didn't say a word. She wanted to say, *Hold the line, I'll call Homayoon*, but it was as if she was paralyzed and couldn't move or speak.

Sadika continued, "Encourage him to come back. I'll interview him. This job is his. Mr. Homayoon is a good doctor. It's a pity that here he stays unemployed and useless. "

Zari said, "I understand, Ms. Doctor."

Sadika laughed loudly and said, "I'm not a doctor the way you think, but I got my Ph.D. But not like Mr. Homayoon. Mr. Homayoon is a real doctor. You simply call me Sadika or Sadigheh, as you like. My sisters also had to change their names. You know, because of the difficulty of the pronunciation."

Zari said, "I understand."

Sadika said, "Batool became Beti, Razieh has become Rozi, and Khadieh become Kadija ..."

Zari didn't listen anymore. The phone's receiver in her hand, she went to the bedroom where Homayoon was still sleeping. Then Zari went back to the living room. Sadika had finished the list of her sisters' names.

Zari said, "Thanks a lot."

Sadika said, "I have to be thankful to you. You helped me a lot when I was just a newcomer. I'll never forget that. Without your help I wouldn't be in the place that I am now. So, tomorrow, send Mr. Doctor to me. The job is Mr. Homayoon's. We have eaten your bread and salt. My father had made me promise that—

Zari said again, "Thank you very much."

Sadika said goodbye and hung up. Zari looked at the receiver in her hand and went to the bedroom, as if she still had the voice of Sadika with her. She sat at the edge of the bed and put her hand on Homayoon's shoulder and shook him.

"Why are you sleeping without a coverlet? Do you want to get sick and be a burden on me? Don't we have enough misery?"

Homayoon still sleepy, said nothing.

Zari showed the telephone to Homayoon and said, "Sadika was on the phone, I mean Sadigheh. She is a nice woman. You were angry with her without a reason."

Homayoon still lay on the bed, staring at Zari and the phone.

Zari said, "She told me that the job is yours. Tomorrow you should go and she will do the interview. Her father had encouraged her to hire you."

Homayoon said, "Her father? What is her father doing here?"

Zari said, "Get up. Don't be so stubborn. Let's go and have dinner. Poor Goli fell asleep crying. With your bad mood, you are making me impatient, too. The poor woman wants to help."

Homayoon sat, and referring to the telephone asked, "Who were you talking to?"

"Weren't you sleeping?"

"Answer my question."

Zari showed the phone to Homayoon and said, "I told you. It was Sadika, I mean the same Sadigheh. She told me that she had told her father about what happened today, and her father said that she should hire you."

"Her father? You mean Mostafa the security man?"

"Well, yes. In Iran he was Mostafa the security man and here, he's the father of six doctors. What's the problem with that? Everyone isn't like us, sliding from up to down. Some have gone from down to up. And it's better to forget about being so stubborn and accept the job. Forget that one day Sadika was Sadigheh. Me, too, I'll forget it. You see that I can't call her Sadigheh anymore. She has become Sadika. What is the problem with it? We shouldn't stick to our ancestors' identity, which is worthless here."

"So what's the value here?"

"I don't know. To have bread on our table and our child not going to school with an empty stomach. And you would be better not being so upset. Our time to be 'somebody' is over. We should think about Goli. Poor thing, she fell asleep still crying. She had been happy thinking that her father would bring her pastry."

Homayoon got up from the bed and went to the living room. Zari followed him and said, "Tell me that tomorrow you'll go, get the job and come back with a box of pastry. Forget about family and ancestors in Iran and things like that. This kind of …"

Homayoon went to the washroom. Zari set the table. She turned the lamp over the dining table on. When Homayoon sat at the table, Zari said again, "Tell me that tomorrow you will go and talk to Sadika. She is a nice woman. At least we are from the same land and we can talk the same language and understand each other better."

Homayoon swallowed his food and said, "Let's see." And then he asked, "What did Sadika say?"

Zari started to report what Sadika had told her. Then she remembered what Sadika had told her: "You said when you saw Sadika you left the building, but Sadika was saying that—"

Homayoon said, "I thought when she saw me, she left the room."

"Why did you make such lies? You just wanted me to believe your words, and now I feel guilty?"

Homayoon said, "If you were there, you would have done the same, too."

Zari pondered. If she had been there, would she really have done the same?

She remembered the names of Sadika's sisters but she just thought of one of them and said, "Batool isn't a difficult name to pronounce. Why did she change it?"

Homayoon asked, "What are you talking about?"

Zari looked at her plate; it was almost untouched. She looked at Homayoon, whose face showed satisfaction and joy: satisfaction from the food filling his stomach and joy from the news that Zari had given him.

Zari stood up to collect the dishes. Homayoon said, "You sit down, I'll wash the dishes."

Zari went and sat on the sofa.

ACKNOWLEDGEMENTS

First of all, I have to thank Lynn Cunningham who edited my manuscript. I'm really in debt to her. My special thanks goes to Luciana Ricciutelli, who accepted my manuscript. Her death was a great shock and sorrow for me.

I have to thank Rebecca Rosenblum for her expertise in editing and having patience with me. I really appreciate her help and her editing.

Also, I have to thank Chandra Wohleber for her help.

Finally, I have to tell Renée Knapp that during these years that I have been working with Inanna Publications it has always been a great joy for me to work with her.

Credit: Syroos Mohsenzadeh

Mehri Yalfani was born in Hamadan, Iran. She graduated from Tehran University with a master's degree in electrical engineering. Mehri immigrated to Canada in 1987. She has published numerous books in Farsi as well as in English, most recently the novel *A Palace in Paradise* (2019) and the short story collection *The Street of Butterflies* (2017). She lives and writes in Toronto. www.yalfani.com